Indian Country

Incident at Big Pine

By
Michael Max Darrow

Dedication

This book is dedicated to my children:
Tatiana, Saige and Cheyenne,
Of whom I am Very Proud.

To the Reader

This book is a work of fiction. Although the characters and events of this story are not true, it does reflect many of the author's true life experiences in regards to his career in law enforcement, with people of the First Nations and in practicing Native American spirituality.

The author wishes to convey to you, dear reader, that his sole intent in penning this novel is to entertain. No offense to any person, organization, location or religion is intended.

Table of Contents

Clean Break

M ike Taylor stood in front of his locker for the last time. It was probably the final time he would make that drive to the Santa Ana Police Department as well. So far he hadn't encountered anybody. It was between shifts and he'd entered the department via the back door, empty gym bag in hand. This was bittersweet to be sure, but it had to be done. He'd resigned upstairs the day before but waited for this off time today to go back and empty out what remained in his locker. Sure, there was a lot of equipment that belonged to the department that he'd already returned, badge and ID among them, but the stuff he'd collected after ten years along with uniforms, Sam Brown gun belt that he'd purchased with his own money, extra clothing, boots and an old crusty towel had to go. He stuffed everything in his bag. The towel definitely stunk.

He zipped the bag shut and was about to make his getaway when he heard one of the locker room doors open and footsteps coming down a side aisle. *Rats*, he thought. He wasn't going to get out of here unmolested afterall.

"Mikey D! I thought that was you on the back camera," Sergeant Jim Callaway said after rounding the corner and coming to a stop, "I can't believe you're quitting! Mike, we went through the academy together."

"What are you, Station Sergeant tonight? I know you hate that," Mike said.

"Stop changing the subject. Is this all because you were passed up for sergeant? Or because of Maria Vasques? Or both?"

Mike smiled and picked up his bag to leave.

"I'm never going to be a sergeant here, you know that. I'm not one of the *golden boys*. And sure, I guess Maria has a little to do with it too. Seeing her in the halls and having her send me on barking dog calls isn't fun. But I got hired in South Dakota as a sergeant and with my college degree there's room for advancement. Police work is police work. Different codes to memorize is all. I'll miss you and the money we make here but I need a fresh start. I never fit in here anyway," he replied.

"Man, I can't freaking believe it. What a loss. I mean what's wrong with patrol? We have a lot of great career patrolmen here and you are one of them. If you change your mind I'm sure they will take you back in a heartbeat. Weren't you Officer of the Month just last month?"

"Two months ago, yeah. I'll miss you too. Hey, I'll stay in touch, I'm just a text away. I'm just glad to be able to use my Lakota a little more often and Spanish a little less often."

"Oh yeah, you speak Lakota and what about your weekly Sweat Lodge at the Indian Reservation in Temecula? You love that!" Jim asked.

"I'll find a lodge. I just need to get out of the big city, get under the stars. This place is wearing me out, I feel it in my soul."

"Alright, I get it, be a resident deputy, take your car home at night, slower pace, big sky country and all that..."

"Big sky is Montana Jimmy boy," Mike said.

"Oh, right. When you leaving?" Jim asked.

"Today. The Tahoe is packed and the Airstream is ready to go. I did the walk through at my apartment and turned in the keys this morning. I just gotta go pick up Max from my dad's house in Tustin and I'm on the road."

"Wow, you're really serious if you're taking that mutt of yours too?"

"Yup, no hard feelings," Mike said.

"Well, I'm still pretty upset about it. Kelley will be upset too when I tell her. We'll miss you coming over for barbeques and free meals with that dog of yours."

Mike smiled and shook his old friend's hand and walked back out and up to the back door with Jim behind him. They bid each other farewell again as he left.

It was a weird feeling to leave a job he loved. It didn't seem real. He chuckled knowing he still had a full set of unit and door keys in his pocket that no one ever cared to ask for. He could go jump in a patrol car and drive away with it and no one would be the wiser he thought. This lent to the surreal feeling he was having.

His dad was still at work when he arrived. He backed

up to his eighteen foot Airstream trailer and hooked up. He could see Max, his Australian Cattle Dog looking out the front window at him. The dog was wagging his tail but was looking on nervously, perhaps thinking his master was driving away without him, who could tell…

"I'm comin'!" he said, looking towards the dog.

He went and got Max and loaded him up in the front cab, and they left, the house he grew up in fading away in his rearview mirror while Jose Feliciano sang "California Dreamin'" on the radio.

He drove for several days at a leisurely pace, stopping at rest areas for Max to relieve himself or, chase rabbits and squir-rels, resulting in him running after Max and having a good laugh. Mike and his dog had a good relationship. Mike had raised the dog from a pup. They seemed to know what the other was thinking. They stopped at Good Sam and KOA-approved RV campgrounds every afternoon. He wasn't in a hurry. He liked to take his time, listen to songs of the sixties and seventies and drive eight to ten hours a day, depending on how he felt, leaving plenty of time for sleep and study. He had been reading up on the penal code sections, radio and vehicle codes for the state of South Dakota.

Mike spent a good amount of time reflecting on his years of service at the police department and his military service before that. He got angry with himself every time he thought of Maria. He had broken the cardinal rule of dating where you work, and he was still kicking himself for it. *Don't dip your pen in company ink.* How many times had he been told that, told others that. Yet he had broken it, and it had cost him. He just couldn't resist a petite brown-haired, brown-eyed girl. When they broke up after three years of dating, it got real uncomfortable. It seemed all of dispatch had turned against him. They stuck together, those dispatchers. The only time Mike Taylor felt free was when he was in a patrol car or at a sweat lodge in the womb of Mother Earth beating a drum, sweating and praying. He also knew he was the anomaly, a six foot two, blond haired, blue eyed white boy that followed Native American spirituality.

He timed his drive to coincide with the office hours of the Veterans of Foreign Wars (VFW) post near the Pine County Sheriff's Office, where he was to report to work. The VFW was a good resource for veterans much like the American Legion. In fact, if one was a member of the VFW he, or she for that matter, could go to the other. They honored each other's membership cards. This particular post allowed overnight parking of RVs and motorhomes of its members. Since Mike was a card carrying member of the VFW, having served in the Middle East, he planned to take advantage of the parking situation until he could find a more permanent spot. Other fraternal organizations like the Elks, Masons and Moose had similar benefits for members. His dad was a lifetime Elk and had been after him for years to join, but Mike didn't like the haughtiness of the rituals. At a VFW post you could find fellow veterans, no suit or rituals were needed, and the beer was always cold and cheap.

Mike checked into the post after parking in the back lot. It was fenced, so that was a plus. He was told he could only stay for four days at a time due to some local ordinance, but after a day could come back. He had to be in the lot at 2 a.m. daily because the gate was closed and locked from 2 a.m. to 6 a.m. every day. The post itself was small, consisting mostly of a bar and a meeting room that was dual purpose, being a meeting room and a dining room. They had a small kitchen and served burgers and sandwiches but had sit-down dinners every Friday and Saturday night, sponsored by either the Auxiliary or the Officer members. He was just glad this post had the bar as some are dry.

The sheriff's office was about a twenty-minute drive. After dropping his Airstream he put Max in the cab and they headed out to go get his uniforms and equipment. He had to cut across a portion of the big Lakota Indian reservation but there were plenty of county roads and even a state road going right through the Big Pine Indian reservation, often just referred to as the b*ig rez.*

From what he could see it looked like a desolate place with a lot of run-down houses and trailers and broken-down cars sitting where they had taken their last breath. They had some towns and clinics of their own but his route didn't take him through any. He knew curiosity would get to him eventually and he would visit the towns, museums and gift shops. He wondered what the policy was on driving a county vehicle on the rez. He guessed he would find out in due time. There were no gates or guards on this reservation. It was too huge for that, being a few thousand square miles. There were just signs on the highways telling a driver he was either entering or leaving the Indian Reservation.

The only Lakota people Mike had ever known was his next-door neighbor who'd introduced him to the Lakota star lodge, or inipi, and the language and prayers of the people when he was ten years old. He'd been hooked ever since and met other Native Americans, friends and relatives of his neighbor Phil over the years. This was Mike's first time on a real reservation, not just the fancy casino resorts sprinkled all over California. No, this was the real deal, poverty on a grand scale. He'd been told about it–Native Americans that don't work but survive on their monthly government checks below the national poverty level. He was prepared, but still, it was shocking. And he had only seen a small fraction of it so far.

Mike parked out front and walked in through the lobby door with Max off leash. He didn't like leashes. A female police service officer, or whatever they were called at a sheriff's department, was working the front desk and called the watch commander, who came out front. Mike noticed no secure doors at all. This was definitely the country. In big cities like Santa Ana, people were buzzed into the front desk area where there were always at least a few armed officers working with the non-sworn police service officers, and all doors leading into and out of the inner workings of the department were metal and electrically secured and controlled.

The lieutenant shook his hand and looked down at Max.

"That dog police trained?"

"Adlerhorst trained, sir," Mike said.

"No shit! I was just kidding, wow! He could come in handy around here. We only have a few dogs. Come on, I'll take you to the storeroom. All your stuff is boxed up. I gotta hear about this big city California copper coming out here to the sticks!"

He followed the lieutenant, who'd introduced himself as Lieutenant Bob Hicks, to a storeroom while answering all his questions about why he quit his job in California and why on earth he would pick South Dakota to work in and asked how much money he'd made monthly in Los Angeles, California.

Mike corrected the lieutenant on location, telling him he'd worked in Santa Ana, that it was much like Los Angeles in crime but not as big, being only twenty-seven square miles. He explained as simply as possible, without getting into personal details, that he wanted a fresh start and that he spoke the Lakota dialect and wanted to go somewhere he could use it. He then had to explain briefly why he spoke Lakota.

Lieutenant Hicks gave him the big cardboard box with his name on it and he opened it up on the floor, finding uniforms and complete gun belt, ballistic vest, cuffs and a set of keys, flat badge in a leather basketweave case with an ID card with his name on it but no photo, yet to be laminated.

The lieutenant told him he could wear denim bluejeans in the field if the pants were too long. They were pretty informal on pants; they just had to be clean and no stylish rips like the kids like to wear these days.

"What about a gun? That's a Glock holster. Do you have a Glock?" Hicks asked.

"Yessir, I told them I have a Glock and magazines with military ball ammo. They said that was fine. I just need to have the armorer approve it eventually."

"You're scheduled for swing shift on Friday. Just come in an hour early around 1 p.m., and I'll have him available to check it. What about a locker? Most deputies come in already dressed, especially our resident deputies, whenever we see them. I don't know what's available, but I can check the assignment book. Where are you staying?" he asked.

"At the VFW post in Shaking Aspen for a few days until I can find someplace a little more permanent to park my Airstream, maybe someplace closer to the station?"

"Talk to Captain Trask. He's the one that recommended you to the sheriff for hire. He lives in Oak Glen, just up the hill. He has ten acres or so...all nice high pasture land in the foothills. But there's lots of places to park a trailer out here. It's pretty wide open country just not on the rez; you'll never see your trailer again! And always lock the tongue. Indians tend to help themselves to RVs and trailers. Once it's on the rez no one is going to look for it."

"I'll talk to him. I'm supposed to check in with him before my first roll call anyway. Hey, what's the rule on driving across the reservation? I noticed there are state and county roads going across it." Mike asked.

"Stay off the rez without telling dispatch and getting watch commander approval. They don't like us much and the rez police are not that cooperative either, even though we're all law enforcement. Then again you speak their language so maybe you'll have better luck?"

"Good to know," Mike said as they reached the front lobby. He said goodbye to the lieutenant and the police service officer working the front desk and left, Max trotting by his side.

Mike drove back to the VFW post. He noticed an interesting looking little diner along the way called the Thunderbird Cafe. There were several cars and pickup trucks in the lot so he figured it must be good. He made a mental note of it. He wasn't in Orange County with a restaurant on every block, Starbucks on every corner anymore.

He unloaded his box of goodies and looked everything over a bit closer, spreading things out on the kitchen table of his Airstream. The uniforms were all used except for one shirt that appeared new, with fresh shoulder patches, sergeant's chevrons and cloth badge. No name tapes yet; they were probably ordered. He decided to keep the one good shirt for his first day, first impressions and all that. Still, it was going to be weird wearing a tan uniform top with a five point star and green trousers after so many years of wearing an oval LAPD-style badge and navy blue uniforms. Even the leather was foreign to him. It was all a basketweave pattern. He wore plain black leather in Santa Ana. The leather gear was all used but in good condition as were the Peerless brand handcuffs.

Deputy in a box, he thought. Pretty straightforward and simple. It was refreshing really, thinking back on all he went through to start work in Santa Ana. That process had taken weeks–everything new, classes, range qualifications, fingerprinting for the FBI, the works. He was a country deputy sergeant now.

Pine County was a little under two thousand square miles. A tad bigger than the twenty-seven square miles of Santa Ana, California. Yet the population was less. More big open spaces, vast expanses of land with most of the population in small cities and unincorporated towns. It was going to take some getting used to. Santa Ana was densely populated; catching bad guys was like shooting fish in a barrel. He could find one or two occupied stolen vehicles to chase every day, with dispatched calls back-to-back, especially on weekends and holidays, not to mention Halloween, the Fourth of July and New Year's. It was like a war zone. Full moons were always full of surprises as well. That was the nature of police work in the big city.

No, there was no orientation ride-a-long and no months of training with a training officer. He was jumping in with both feet, expected to know how to go out there, different uniform or not, and be not only a trained and experienced law enforcement officer but a first line supervisor meeting his crew, not knowing who or how many that would be, in just a few days. Mike Taylor found it both stimulating and challenging.

Day One

Mike checked in two hours early, wearing the new shirt and ballistic vest but opting for a good pair of his own Wrangler blue jeans as the uniform pants were all loose and way too long. He wore his own black Army issue combat boots; it was a veteran thing. He also had two as-of-yet unauthorized back up weapons and a sharp clip knife in his front pocket. Some things remained the same after all he'd been through, like the single handcuff key he carried in his left rear pocket just in case someone ever got the jump on him and restrained him with his own cuffs.

On the way up to Captain Trask's office on the second floor he got a lot of looks from people, both deputies and non-sworn staff: clerks, secretaries and police service officers. He was polite, saying hello whenever he could. He saw a few dark complected faces but didn't try any Lakota on them: they could be Hispanic and that would be embarrassing. He'd hold the language skill in reserve, he thought to himself. He didn't want to come off as a show-off or know-it-all. No one likes a know-it-all.

Captain Trask was on the phone but motioned for Mike to come in. The door to his office stood wide open and Mike took that as a good sign. In Santa Ana the Captains, Deputy Chiefs and Chief that had their doors always closed were just that: closed to any input from the troops. The chief even had his own personal secretary. Mike wondered if the Sheriff of the County had his own secretary, but he'd yet to meet him or even see his office and he only knew what he looked like from the framed photo of him in the lobby and on department letterhead from his office.

"Sergeant Taylor," Trask said, hanging up the phone, "I see you went with the Levi option, pants too long?"

"Yessir," Mike said, smiling out of nervousness.

"I'm glad you stopped by early, I was going to come find you, put a bug in your ear before roll call. So, what's your plan for your first meeting of the third watch men and ladies, you have two, one is trouble. But, we'll get to that."

"Well Sir, I need to have the armorer check my weapons. Lieutenant Hicks has him coming by the watch commander's office at thirteen hundred and then I was going to put my posse box in a unit after getting some forms from the report room and then get the roll from the watch commander, go and hold a roll call." Mike said, rambling nervously, having already planned out the events in his mind.

"Weapons?" Trask asked.

Mike hesitated.

"I have a Walther PPK/S in my back pocket and a two shot hold-out Deringer in my front Left pocket if I'm on my back fighting for control of my service weapon with my Right hand and can't get to the Walther. I would have brought my AR-15 but I didn't know the rules on that yet?"

Trask's eyebrows raised, "Wow, at ease soldier. You won't need all that here and no on the hardware. You have a shotgun in your SUV, the Ford Explorer is the sergeant's vehicle. There are extra road flares and equipment in there and four wheel drive. The deputies have the Crown Vics. Your backup weapons are fine. I never carried one but I understand your training and experience. I was a cold war Marine. Never fired a shot. But I know you have, and I know you've been in a few on duty shootings as well. Mike, it's a little more laid back out here in the old West. But you'll get used to that...in time. Now, what is your get to know me speech for the troops?"

"Well sir, I was going to hold roll call and then tell them about my background and that I'm not here to change anything or judge them based on where I came from. I'm just going to observe for a while and I'd appreciate their help in getting to know the lay of the land and new code numbers."

"Good, keep it short. I like the *observe* bit. That's what you should do. This is the country. Think low speed, high drag. I know that's the opposite of what you're used to but these guys will be judging you. Some of them were passed up by your hire and there will be resentment, Deputy Yancy Rivera being one of them. She has been on an arrest rampage ever since. Come see me Monday and tell me how it's going, and good luck!" he finished.

"Oh, one more thing Cap. I'm looking for a place to park my Airstream for a while till I get oriented. I'm at the VFW Post but they have this four day limit thing?" he asked hopefully.

The Captain took a Post-It note pad and wrote down an address and phone number on it.

"Here's my address and phone number. I have ten acres. We can find you a spot and run an extension cord out to you. No sewage so you'll have to go dump when you're full. Stay as long as you like," he smiled, handing Mike the Post-It note.

Mike said goodbye and went down to the report room where he'd left his posse box. He wondered if the deputies out here used a posse box or even knew what one was. It was a simple enough contraption, a big black plastic box with a bent metal bar that allowed an officer to hang it over the passenger seat. It had everything he needed for a ten hour shift in it. Blank report forms for everything from simple information reports to crime and incident reports, accident reports and continuation forms. They didn't have as many forms as Santa Ana. That was nice. He also picked up a ticket book and put it in his aluminum framed ticket book holder that matched his aluminum report writing clipboard.

His posse box already had what he called the essentials in it: extra shotgun rounds; double 00 buckshot, extra box of 9mm rounds, his flashlight and charger, a phone charger, disposable medical gloves and surgical masks for dead body calls with the secret ingredient, a small bottle of the menthol aftershave Aquavelva. Just a drop inside the mask and the smell of death was gone. He also had a few water bottles in there just in case. And baby wipes. Always baby wipes.

Mike Taylor was a product of his training and experience. He'd been trained by cops from the 70's and 80's and they had been trained by cops from the 60's. That handcuff key in the back pocket, that was an old school safety precaution. He would probably be the only one out here that did that. The contents of his posse box had shrunk over the years, ditching the first aid kit and various writing utensils and templates for everything from writing in block print to making little figures for traffic accident reports. He'd made them so many times he didn't need a template anymore. Like he'd retired the fancy Cross Pen set everyone wore upon graduation from the academy, and the nice leather notepad holder that was just too heavy and hard to get out of the top pocket when taking notes of a crime or citizen contact. A disposable Bic pen and a 25 cent note pad worked just fine.

Finally he stuffed some generic fill-in-your-name business cards in his other top pocket that also held a small pupil chart for determining the size of a person's pupils when suspected of being under the influence of certain drugs, and headed out to the rear parking lot to find the Ford Explorer.

It was nothing to write home about. Just another,

slightly older, Ford Explorer Police Package. They must have two, he reasoned, or the second watch (dayshift) sergeant was off today. He had no way of knowing, but there was no equipment in it so he put his in, checked all the lights and searched the back seat for contraband. He had found discarded needles, knives and guns before. Mike knew it was pretty embarrassing to have been the officer that previously used that car when a weapon was found. Not to mention scary too. That weapon was dropped by a subject placed in the backseat. It could have been used on that officer. That's why it was equally important to search a police unit after your shift as well.

In the back of the Explorer was a box with extra equipment in it: flares, road vests and yellow emergency blankets, more often used to cover dead bodies than actually warm victims, first aid kit, case of water and the all important jumper cables. Some departments put a second battery in their units to run the emergency lights when the car or SUV was turned off with the lights on for long periods of time at accidents or other events. Santa Ana did not. Running your battery down happens often. The newer LED lights were easier on the system drain but it still happened.

Mike made it back inside and to the watch commander's office just in time to meet deputy Grant, the department armorer. He checked each one of Mike's guns and said they were fine – that simple. No paperwork, no firing required. Another refreshing part of being a country deputy. He asked about monthly range qualification and was informed it was quarterly here. Deputy Grant left and Lieutenant Hicks had Mike sit down as he got the roll call sheet out and went over it with him.

"So, how did it go with the Captain? Did you ask him about parking your rig on his property?" Hicks asked him, as he turned the roll call form around on his desk, facing Mike.

"Yeah, no problem. He gave me his address and phone number. But I'm not going to rush right up there if you know what I mean. I'll give it a few days. Hey, what's with the four day limit on parking an RV or Trailer in this county anyways?"

"Well, that has to do with the Indians too, like I said, they tend to do what they want. The story is that many moons ago some Indians decided to park off the rez and make their own little communities in the county."

"Well, that makes sense. We had a lot of goofy muni codes in Santa Ana too that had their origins in previously perceived odd behaviors. Did you know that Indians prefer to be called Native American or Indigenous? They find the word Indian offensive," Mike said casually, looking at the roll call sheet and noting he had about twelve deputies that didn't have an R next to their name. He figured those were the resident deputies.

"No kidding. I've heard that before, sure. But, their signs all say Indian Reservation so I figured it's like the black rappers using the N word but you know, you and I can't say it. Now, the deputies with the R next to their names are not coming in to roll call. Well, sometimes they do. But don't expect it. I leave at 5 p.m. and then you are on your own. The station is locked up. There is a recording on the phone to call 911 if it's an emergency and all other business and reports in person or over the phone are from 8 to 5. Dispatch has the numbers of the brass in the event of an emergency or major incident. I don't know what you are used to?"

"So", Mike ventured to ask, "there are no Crime Scene Investigators or Civilian Accident Investigators on after 5 p.m.?"

The lieutenant smiled at that.

"I don't know what you were expecting out here but we don't have any of those. Detectives do their own CSI, and deputies, the ones that aren't lazy, take photos on their phones and forward them too. We have a couple of traffic guys that work dayshift, but they'll come out on a major incident if you ask for them. They've been to school for that. A few deputies carry fingerprint kits, but you know, no one wants to get that Lightning Powder on them or in their eyes. It's nasty stuff."

Mike was surprised. This really was the wild west out here.

"Good to know. I'll have to build a new print kit. I have no problem lifting prints on burglary and other calls. The

Orange County crime lab back home used to get lots of hits on my prints that led to arrests, I turned mine in when I left. I used it on graveyard shift mostly. We had civilians for CSI and Accidents on the other shifts. Guess I was lucky!"

"You'll be fine. That's why the Captain pushed for your hire. You have a lot of experience, certainly more schooling than me and probably more than Captain Trask himself!"

"Wow. Guess I just took that stuff for granted."

"You were in a big city with lots of revenue. This is a county without...a lot of things. I'll wander down for roll call if you don't mind. I want to hear this and keep the troops in line. I hope you have thick skin because you are an outsider and the rat pack is on. Expect a lot of pranks at your expense until they get to know you," the lieutenant finished.

Mike got up with the roll call sheet and made his way downstairs to the roll call room next to the locker room and a very dusty old gym full of rusted and broken equipment.

There was a long table outside the multipurpose room used for roll call among other things. A coffee vending machine stood nearby along with a soda vending machine. Coffee was only fifty cents which he thought was a bargain coming from the land of a Starbucks at five bucks a shot. He fed in two quarters and watched as a little paper cup with little images of playing cards on the sides was dispensed. He recognized them immediately. There was a similar coffee machine in the bowels of the Santa Ana

Police Department back in his high school days when he was an Explorer Scout. That's when he fell in love with police work, looking up to the officers he rode along with on weekend nights. He retrieved his black coffee and lifted it high in the air to see the hidden hole card on the bottom of the cup. He always figured one could gamble with these cups but he'd never seen anyone do it. He sat down at the table and waited for his deputies to arrive, eager to see who was punctual and who was a last minute Lulu. This information told one a lot about people and their habits, plus he wanted some informal time to meet arriving deputies.

The coffee was terrible.

Deputies began to arrive, most already dressed, but wearing light windbreaker-like jackets over their uniforms and carrying bags. They all went into the locker room for a time, coming out in uniform with either a report box or briefcase in their hands. Most were white with two females, one hispanic, whom he knew had to be Yancy Rivera, and a few male hispanic or indigenous deputies. The females did not go into the locker room and sat their belongings along the wall of the roll call room. Yancy didn't even look at him and went directly inside and sat down out of sight. The other deputies smiled and said hello or asked if he was the new sergeant, which was obvious, but they were just making polite conversation. He greeted them all, introducing himself as Mike Taylor.

A few of the deputies that were early went back upstairs

with their equipment, hoping to snag a unit not in use. These were the faces Mike would remember when he needed a deputy or two to go in service early if the call arose, which was bound to happen.

Five minutes before the hour, Mike got up to go into the room. Everyone was waiting on him as they all got up, eleven or so, and followed him inside. Deputy Rivera was sitting dead center in the front row, right in front of the lectern. This wasn't going to be comfortable, he thought...

He looked over his notes taking his position at the lectern. He had called up to dispatch for anything that was going on and had introduced himself to the two dispatchers on duty. Lori, the dispatcher he was talking to, gave him the plate and description of an old stolen Buick that had been seen coming off the rez with four young male adults inside about two hours ago. There were also two theft calls pending. He thanked her and said if they needed a food run to give him a call. He knew that a happy dispatcher was a good thing.

One minute before the hour, the lieutenant came in and said good afternoon to everyone and sat down in a chair near the door in case he needed to make a hasty exit.

Exactly on the hour, Mike Taylor started his first roll call as a sergeant at a new department. He noticed that the deputies varied in age and build and sat scattered about the room, most of the older veteran deputies with big bellies sat in the back row, two hispanic looking officers that looked like twins sat right next to each other. All in all it was a typical looking affair.

He began by calling everyone's name. Each answered differently, from the familiar "Here," to "Yup," to "Yeo," and Deputy Rivera answered, "Present Sergeant." She was sitting upright at a military seated attention, a Marine Corps pin on her left breast pocket flap. After that he said there were two theft calls pending and gave them the BOLO (Be On the Lookout) info on the reported stolen Buick. Then he gave his speech.

"Before I get started, I understand there are a few of you that were not promoted due to my hiring and I apologize for that. I had no control over that and I know what that feels like having been passed up for sergeant twice before."

He made the briefest of eye contact with Deputy Rivera before continuing.

"Now, as for who I am and why I'm here, I started in law enforcement as a police explorer scout with the city of Santa Ana. After high school I enlisted in the United States Army where my plan was to be an MP. The Army had other plans for me and I ended up in the Mechanized Infantry and did a tour in Iraq. After the Army I went back home and was hired by the Santa Ana PD where I worked patrol, mostly all on the graveyard shift, while attending college and getting my Bachelors in Criminal Justice. I also attended Intoxilyzer Operator school, Traffic Accident school, General Investigations school, Auto Theft school, and the two week intensive Drug Recognition Expert course at the Los Angeles Sheriff's Academy.

"As I said, I was passed up for promotion for reasons I won't get into and started looking elsewhere. I speak Lakota and Spanish so I thought this area was a good fit. I was a Staff Sergeant in the Army and I have a pretty laid back leadership style. I'm not here to tell anyone what to do, so don't make me. You are all trained law enforcement officers and I'll hold you to that. I understand this department does not employ report analysts and that is also my job so I'll get to know your style of police work by reading your reports and citations which you put in my box. Other than that, I'm sure you will all get to know me in time."

"Ugh, citations too?" a younger deputy said. There were a few other groans at that as well.

"Yes, cites too. I want to see who my traffic guys, or gals, are. Your Field Contact cards you can turn in directly to records. I don't need to see those. I expect you to call in all car stops and follow if you are able."

"How do you speak Lakota?" Deputy Rivera asked.

"Well, that's a story for another time. We need to get out there. Suffice to say I grew up practicing Lakota spirituality from a young age. I also grew up in a city where eighty percent of the population spoke Spanish, so I learned that too."

He noticed that the two twins, who were indeed twins, were putting something in their mouths as he spoke. They now sat back and smiled at him with plastic vampire fangs.

And so it begins, he thought. These two were okay. They were trying to get him to break character and laugh or react in some way. He looked right at them and winked without smiling.

"Let's be safe out there," Mike finished, gathering up his roll call sheet and his notes. The deputies began filing out.

He stepped down and handed the roll call sheet to the lieutenant who whispered, "Good luck," as he walked out of the room.

Only Deputy Rivera was left, sitting at her seat and looking at him.

"Something on your mind, Marine?" he asked her.

"I was fully prepared to hate you but I guess you do have more training than me. But I do also have a Bachelor's Degree. The Lakota is killer though. I obviously speak Spanish but how the hell do you speak Lakota? I mean you look like you should be surfing in Hermosa Beach! No disrespect intended," she said.

Mike smiled at her before answering, "I grew up going to Lakota-style sweat lodge every weekend. My neighbor was from the rez. He taught me. I liked it enough to continue into adulthood but there weren't a lot of opportunities in the Army. I resumed after."

"Huh, that's crazy. I can see why the Sheriff hired you then. I'll see you out there," she said, as she got up and gathered up her clipboard. "You should wear an Army Pin on your pocket. All us vets do that around here."

"I will, thank you. I'm still learning what is allowed and not allowed," he replied as she smiled and walked out to find a unit.

She was cute, but she was wearing a wedding band and he had learned that lesson. He took a deep breath and went upstairs to go in service. This was the *riding a bicycle* part of law enforcement. Go out there and do some police work, answer calls for service and for the first time in his law enforcement career, answer calls for a supervisor as well. Still, he thought to himself, a pretty good first roll call.

The Thunderbird Cafe

It was just past midnight on the day before Mike's first roll call when John LaVoy found an open door on his rounds as the night shift security guard at the twin warehouses of L & M Logistics. L & M were government contractors, shipping and supplying big ticket items to the reservation. The warehouses were just inside the rez off of route 6, a few miles from the tribal government area.

"Oh, I'll have to call you back hun, I found an unlocked door," he said to his wife.

"Don't go inside! You told me you're not supposed to go inside. Just call your supervisor," she said, concerned.

"Yeah, yeah, I'll call you back," he said, hanging up and putting his cell phone in his pocket.

John stood there in the doorway listening for any movement inside. He didn't hear anything after about a minute, other than his own nervous breathing and heartbeat so he decided to go inside even though they were all told not to. What could it hurt, he thought. Probably just a door left open when they closed. He had worked here for over two years and there were a lot of shipments coming and going and it was kind of a mystery what L & M was up to. His coworkers had a conspiracy theory that it was some government front and they were really exploiting Native artifacts or minerals they were stealing from the rez, maybe even uranium. The government had illegally drilled for uranium there before. He decided to have a peek first and then call his supervisor.

He walked around for a while looking at big boxes of washers and dryers: the good top of the line industrial kind. He found a shelving unit full of laptop computers and chromebooks, which was odd: they were supposed to go to the schools on the rez. He knew the government was refurbishing a few of the laundromats, but this was a lot of washers and dryers, like hundreds of them. He took a picture of the writing on one of the boxes containing a washing machine including brand, model and serial numbers, then checked the inner office doors which were all locked. He noticed there were cameras in the warehouse that appeared to be working, a little red LED light illuminated on each one. He wandered around for another ten minutes before deciding to go back outside and call his supervisor.

Back outside, he called his boss and told him of the open door. His boss said he would be right down as soon as he could get dressed. He was also a Native American and didn't live far away. John called his wife back and told her to go to bed, that his supervisor was on his way and he would see her in the morning.

Just after hanging up he heard a noise coming from the warehouse behind him.

He looked up as a figure exited the door.

Startled, John took a step back and his hand shot up to his chest in shock as he sucked in a deep breath. Then he recognized the man.

"Oh, it's you! You scared the shit out of me! I didn't know anyone was inside," he said.

A single gunshot rang out and John LaVoy crumpled to the ground with a 9mm bullet in his gut. He did not make it home.

Mike drove around for his first few hours getting used to the area. He made concentric circles, sort of, as much as one can make circles in an area consisting of streets set up in grid squares running either north-south or east-west. He checked on Max, even though he'd worked out a deal with Patty, the daytime bartender at the lodge who would check on the mutt after her shift. She seemed okay, no needle track marks on her arms and had been working there for seven years so Mike figured he could trust her because she was a single mom of three and a Navy vet. He didn't really have anything of value in his Airstream. He didn't believe in keeping expensive stuff. His AR-15 rifle was hidden in a locked compartment in a storage area under the trailer.

Max had his own dog door cut into the front door and Mike carried portable 4 foot wire fencing, which Max could easily clear if he wanted to, and made a 4 foot by 8 foot area in front of the door complete with artificial turf he rolled out. He spoiled the dog, but he was his best friend after all, never broke his heart or stabbed him in the back like so many *buddies* back in Santa Ana. It would take quite a while for Mike to get over that place.

The radio had been silent except for the two theft calls that were dispatched as soon as his deputies started going into service. *County deputies,* he thought, probably off visiting friends or eating or whatever. He'd told them to call in car stops, but they probably weren't. He wasn't going to change things, get them to be more officer safety oriented on his first day. It would be a process. He'd check their citations for date and time of violation and see who was cooperating and who was not.

He was getting hungry and decided to head over to that cafe he'd noted. It was around 1630 hours, that's 4:30pm for civilians, and Mike wanted to beat the dinner crowd. The parking lot was about half full when he pulled in, noticing a Tribal Police SUV parked in the back row by itself. He backed in next to it and walked to the front doors, but couldn't help but notice in his observant police way that a lot of cars were older and had bumper stickers like *Native Pride* or *Honor Student* for the rez middle school. He realized this was a native watering hole. It was located next to a road that led to a side entrance to the rez and a clinic just inside the rez which he was not aware of just yet.

When he went inside many Native Americans near the front door stopped talking and looked his way. It was obvious this big, blonde haired, blue eyed County Deputy Sergeant was not what they were used to seeing in the diner. He looked for a table and the Tribal Policeman, also Native American with his hair in a long black ponytail, made eye contact with him and waved him back to where he was sitting in the last booth, his back against the wall. Well at least he has good officer safety, Mike thought as he headed back to increased looks and a deepening hush.

At the booth just before the Tribal Policeman, an elderly Native American was helping his wife out of the booth and started to assist her with his hand on her elbow towards the door. Mike backed up against the counter so they could pass. He noticed the man was wearing a Vietnam Veteran hat.

"Thank you for your service," Mike said as they passed, the man nodding at him.

As Mike turned to walk past their booth he noticed the man had left his sunglasses on the table. He grabbed them up quickly and turned towards the slow moving couple.

"Uncle," he said in perfect Lakota, "Your glasses!"

The cafe fell completely silent except for the clattering sounds from the kitchen. Even the two waitresses had stopped dead in their tracks to look at Mike.

The man turned and looked at Mike, coming to a stop. Mike walked towards him, holding up his sunglasses and handed them to him.

"Pelameyaya," the older man said, thanking him and nodding, then turned to continue assisting his wife out of the restaurant. He didn't even react to the fact that a white-man, a wasicu (wasi'chu), had just spoken to him in his native tongue.

"Momma, he speaks our language!" said a young girl, sitting with her mother and her aunt.

"What? Y'all never seen a white boy speak Lakota before?" Mike said smiling.

"No," came the response from about five people as he turned back towards the Tribal Policeman. Talk resumed gradually as the people began reacting to what they had just seen, and heard.

"Oh, I've *got to* hear all about this! Have a seat stranger!" the policeman said, motioning for Mike to have a seat.

Mike sat down. He wasn't too comfortable having someone he didn't know watch his back, but he was law enforcement after all…

"Hi. Mike Taylor. What's good here?" he said smiling, and offered his hand to the policeman, who looked to be about ten years older than him.

The man looked at his hand and up at Mike's face for a moment before accepting it.

"Hobby War Club, where the hell did you come from? And how do you speak Lakota?"

"Well, that's kind of a long story so I'll give you the Readers Digest version. I'm from Santa Ana, California, born and raised. After a hitch in the Army I went home to be a local copper for ten years before getting hired by Pine County. Today is actually my first day. I started going to inipi at my neighbor's house when I was ten, been sweating ever since. Kind of sunk in I guess."

A waitress came over and looked at Mike with her order pad in hand, eyebrows raised, half expecting the big whiteman to order in Lakota.

"He'll have what I'm having, Jewel," Hobby said.

"Right," she said, and walked away.

"What are we having?" Mike asked.

"Patty melt and fries. Hope ice tea is okay with you?"

"Yeah, that's fine, thank you," Mike said.

"So, your neighbor, he's Lakota then?"

"Yes he is. Long story there too. He said he was a wanted man and had to flee the rez. But Uncle has a lot of stories. His name is Phil Velardi but he says it's not his real name," Mike said.

Hobby noticed Mike had used the Lakota word for uncle when speaking to the old man and was now saying uncle in english when referring to an older Lakota man. He was impressed by Mike's use of respectful words when referring to or speaking to his elders.

The two men began a conversation as their drinks arrived and then their food. They felt each other out with questions and answers, Hobby wanting to know more about why Mike left an obviously higher paying city police job to come out here to the country and how he was starting as a Sergeant. Mike answered all Hobby's questions trying to be brief and asked his own mostly about how the rez works and if it was true that the Tribal Police and the Sheriff's Department didn't get on all that well.

"If we don't get along it's because most deputies think they are better than us. So, you've never actually been to a Lakota, Dakota or other big reservation outside of California have you?"

"Well, no. We have a lot of small reservations in Southern California where I'm from, big casinos and the people do pretty good. A few years back, Uncle was denied a burning permit by a new fire chief and we had to go to his friends lodge on a wealthy rez in Temecula, has one of the biggest and most beautiful casinos you've ever seen, and Uncle stopped lighting the fire at his house eventually and we just went to the rez. Sometimes it was a rainbow lodge, sometimes not. Even sweated with a few movie stars wanting to appreciate Native American culture."

"Sure, I've heard those Luiseno brothers got it going on. So let me ask you this, are you Indian? Do you claim any Indian blood, maybe Cherokee in your background?" he asked.

"No sir, I'm not First Nations. One hundred percent white from England, Ireland and Scotland."

"The enemy. I'd keep that under your hat around here. So do you think you're going to come sweat on the big rez? It's not like going to church, you know. Not all are welcome. How many Native Americans do you think go to lodge? Do you think all the girls are making traditional dresses and dancing at Pow Wows and all the bucks are in lodge on Sunday?" Hobby asked him, a bit of annoyance in his voice.

"No, back home lodge is a rare thing, only a handful of regulars, and I've never been to a Pow Wow. I reckon it's the same here?"

"That's right. Most of my people are poor, most know of the old ways but don't practice, some go to the white churches, pray to Jesus. So don't expect a big welcome to the rez or lodge around here. Maybe not, who knows. I'm pretty sure that by this time tomorrow when you meet me here for dinner you'll be a legend on the rez. I'm gonna bring a few people I want you to meet. For their sake, not yours"

"Oh, we're having dinner tomorrow too? That's cool. Look, I'm not asking for anything. I've been denied lodge a time or two when a Native American showed up to lodge that didn't want to sweat with a white. It's no big deal. It is what it is. I was going to build my own lodge and get my own lava rocks, do my own thing for a while. I've built a few lodges, burned the ribs of a few in a good way too," Mike said.

Hobby looked at Mike for a few seconds.

"I like you white boy. I don't know why. You're an aberration. But, you are respectful. You don't claim to be an Indian and you don't say *Indian*. First Nations you said. That's good. Maybe there is hope for the white man after all," he said and chuckled.

Just then Hobby's radio broke squelch, and a female voice said, "Hobart, are you available?"

"Oh, that's me," he said, reaching over and grabbing the microphone clipped to an epaulet on his shoulder and depressing the side button, "Sergeant War Club is in service."

"Meet Tully over at HQ. We have a suspicious circs call, possible DB," the dispatcher said.

"Oh, a dead body, swell!" he said to Mike, "Good thing I just ate! I gotta go."

Hobart "Hobby" War Club slid out of his seat and stood up and started fishing in his pocket for money.

"I got it. You get next time. You're a sergeant too? Where are your stripes?" Mike asked.

Hobby reached up and felt his collars where his chrome chevrons were usually pinned.

"Darn it, my wife washed my uniform again!" he said, walking out at a quick pace.

Mike finished his fries and went up to the counter to pay. The cashier, a young slightly overweight Lakota girl kept smiling at him, telling him how cool it was that he spoke Lakota and to come back anytime. She brushed her fingers on his palm as she handed him his change.

That was uncomfortable he thought, as he went out to the SUV and got in. He heard a deputy call in a traffic stop and had to punch in the location on his cellphone on a Maps App and started rolling that way. It wasn't far. He was glad for something police-like to do.

An hour later Mike was driving around again, about to pull over a smoking vehicle for exhaust violations when he heard dispatch radio for a deputy and then himself.

"Pine 313, with 301 to follow, a report of a possible dead body on the North side of Route 6, mile marker 53.39. The reporting party is standing bye."

"313 enroute," Mike heard one of the twins respond.

"Pine 301 enroute," Mike said, and placed the mic back in its cradle on the dash.

Finally, some real police work, he thought. Still, in the forefront of his mind he wondered about the call Hobby got at the Thunderbird Cafe. Did the Tribal Police relocate a DB to County land so they wouldn't have to deal with it? No, they wouldn't. He knew where route 6 was so he headed that way. No need to hurry. The dead don't mind.

Deputy Frank Martinez, indeed one of the twins, was

waiting next to his unit alongside the road. As he pulled up behind him, he could see a body some forty yards away next to the reservation fence. Just on the other side of the fence stood two Tribal Policemen, one of them Sergeant War Club.

He activated his rear facing amber flashers, got out, and walked up to Deputy Martinez.

"So, what have you got? I thought the reporting party was standing by?"

"*They* are the re porting party!" Martinez said, pointing at the Tribal Policemen on the other side of the four foot triple strand barbed wire fence.

Hobby waved and smiled when the two deputies looked his way.

"Hau, kola!" Hobby said. "Long time no see!"

"You know him?" Martinez asked.

"I do." Mike smiled, "What have you got? Have you approached the body, confirmed no signs of life and all that? Do you guys, do *we* need to have paramedics roll a tape to confirm no vital signs out here?"

"No, we don't do that this far out, town limits only. We just hold on the pulse for a good minute to confirm death unless they're stinkers: then there's no need. I approached and checked, he's got a bullet hole in his head. Hispanic or Indian. I'll tell you one thing: there are no tracks but mine leading up to the body but there sure is a lot of tracks on the ground on the other side of the fence! I think they dumped it and called us," he added under his breath.

"Let's not jump to conclusions. Someone dumped it but I don't think it was the police. I was with Sergeant War Club when he got the DB call over an hour ago. So…"

Martinez gave Mike a questioning look. Mike figured he was surprised that his new sergeant had already made friends with the Tribal Police which was probably inevitable with him speaking Lakota and practicing Lakota religion. Mike knew he was odd. To a good Catholic boy like Martinez, it must all seem really weird.

"I'll tell you what: you call dispatch on your cell; I don't want this on the radio. Have them call out Homicide and make proper notifications for a murder. I'm going to go talk to the tribal police. I'll step on your tracks."

Martinez walked around and got in his county vehicle as Mike started following the deputy's footprints up to the body of a middle aged man lying face down with a hole in the back of his head. Mike crouched down to get a better look. He could see a little dried blood around the entrance wound and a good chunk of the man's forehead missing above his right eyebrow. This was the exit wound. There was no blood on the ground, so he knew this was not the location of the murder. The body had been dumped here. He noticed a wallet sitting on the man's rump, a South Dakota driver's license sitting right on top.

"Who did the wallet autopsy, you or my deputy?" he said, looking up at War Club.

"Guilty as charged, tampering with evidence, guess

you'll have to come on this side of the fence and arrest me," Hobby said smiling.

The other officer, a tall Native American just smirked and continued to stare at Mike. The man looked mean or stoic or something else Mike couldn't quite parse.

Mike saw the other set of tracks leading up to the body from the reservation side of the fence. They came from right in the middle of a section of wire between two wood posts. He knew this trick from going bird hunting with his father: One man stepped on the middle wire, pushing it down while pulling up on the top wire so the other person could go through.

Mike put the drivers license back in the wallet, noticing there was money in there that had not been taken, and put it back in the dead man's back jeans pocket for the homicide folks to find. He stood up and walked over to the fence, stepping on Hobby's tracks, then veered off them at the fence line to walk over a few feet to stand face to face with the two Tribal Policemen on the other side.

"Who's your friend?" Mike asked, looking at the tall officer whom he figured to be about six-foot-four.

"Oh, this is Tully. Tully, say hello to Sergeant Andy Taylor. Say, how's Opie doing?"

"That's a good one. I guess that was bound to happen now that I'm wearing green and tan and not blue. It's Mike Taylor," he said, reaching over the fence to shake the man's hand.

Tully just stood there with his thumbs tucked in his belt, looking at Mike.

"It's okay cousin, this wasicu speaks Lakota," Hobby said.

Tully just looked over at Hobby like he made a bad joke.

"Yes, I speak Lakota," Mike said in Lakota, then continued, "I don't speak Lakota very well."

Tully's eyes went wide and his head shot back, "What!"

"I was going to tell you about him, had dinner with him today, it's his first day on the job. But, we got this DB call and it slipped my mind. So Mikey, how do you want to handle this? He's obviously one of ours, thrown over the fence, probably by two people swinging him over, but he's on the white man's side of the fence."

"Any tracks or blood on your side that you didn't drive all over? Who called it in?" Mike asked.

"Anonymous," Tully said, finally breaking his silence.

"No blood and there are lots of tracks. This road is a shortcut from a housing area to the gate," Hobby said.

"Well, I have my deputy calling homicide and making all the notifications. You know this man?"

"I know he's Lakota, that's about it. We can go to his house, do the death notification if you want."

"Hold off on that. I don't want to have homicide pissed off at me on my first day. I'll ask them when they get here."

"Who are your people?" Tully asked him suddenly,

off the subject. This was a question one Native American asked another upon meeting sometimes.

Mike looked up at Tully and thought for a moment.

"I'm not First Nations, I'm white. But I follow the Red Road," he said, referring to Lakota spirituality, "So, I guess I don't have *people.*

Tully raised an eyebrow, "How long have you been on the Red Road?"

"Since I was ten years old. Aho, Mitakuye Oyasin," he said, the phrase being a common prayer ending that means roughly, *all my relations,* or, *we are all related.*

"Aho," Tully said then turned questioningly to Hobby.

"Tell you what, slick: We're going to split. If you need me, call me, here's my number," Hobby handed Mike a business card out of his top pocket. "This is going to take hours. We'll look into things on our side, you know, unofficially. You didn't tell us anything."

"Sounds good. See you tomorrow at the Thunderbird, if not sooner," Mike said, walking back on the tracks to his car.

And So It Begins...

Mike was up at 0630 as usual and getting ready for his morning run. Max had already been outside to do his business and was excited to go jogging with his dad. They both went out and Mike did some stretching before setting out at his usual pace. The morning air was crisp and stung his face, making his eyes water. He'd found a street behind the lodge that wasn't busy, leading back to an old industrial and business area that was about a quarter of a mile long, where he and Max could run back and forth a few times. He was looking forward to running in the country again, he thought. He liked to think as he ran. Getting off the pavement would be a big improvement. He planned on moving his trailer up to Captain Trask's property on his days off. Working a four/ten plan had its advantages. The four/ten hour shifts were long, not as long as some departments that did the crazy three/twelve plan, but the three days off instead of the traditional two with the eight hour a day shifts was definitely an advantage. Every weekend was a three day weekend; problem was, it was Tuesday through Thursday. But he was the junior sergeant and that's just how it goes.

His thoughts turned to the day before and the dead body of the Native American man. He thought he would be working overtime as would have been the case back in the big city, but not out here. The one detective that showed up finally at half past nine was very nonchalant with a lot of, "We'll do it in the mornings." Mike wasn't used to that. He was more accustomed to at least two detectives that started working the case immediately: Death notifications, contacting friends and coworkers for interviews, looking for leads and witnesses. As far as he could tell from this old detective with a portly belly, this was an Indian caper that had gotten dumped on the county. This was mostly true; however, Mike thought, someone has lost their life and it was definitely murder–loved ones would be missing this man and would be upset, more so when they were notified of his passing and at the manner of his passing.

No, Mike thought, he hoped Hobby had defied his wishes and notified the family. It was disrespectful not to. If the man was a traditional Lakota his family would want to know and prepare him for the journey. It is part of the grieving process. Although they do not fear death or the underworld like the white man, they do feel sadness. But they know the dead will go to Wakan Tanka (God), in the spirit world where they are free of pain, to the happy hunting grounds as the white man has come to call it which is not entirely accurate.

And so it begins, he thought as he ended his little

thirty minute run and headed back to the VFW at a walk to cool down. He was now a county deputy sergeant and as Sherlock Holmes used to say in the Sir Arthur Conan Doyle books he read as a kid, "The game is afoot!" He was working and he was in it now.

It was a much different set of circumstances for Sergeant War Club and Officer Tully Brown. Hobby was just now getting home and to bed after an all nighter. They had contacted the decedent's wife, who had collapsed in the doorway when she'd opened the door to see the two Tribal Policemen. At the warehouses the gate was open and a truck was gone. Someone had hosed down the loading docks, but now everything was locked up. Something was wrong, she knew it. Something bad had happened. She told them everything she remembered from her husband's last phone call.

War Club had called out his own department's general investigation team and they started working on it immediately. They knew the drill. This would eventually be their crime, unless the county Sheriff refused to hand it over or heaven forbid the almighty FBI was called in. *Famous but Incompetent,* among other backronyms the Native people had for them.

Hobby lay in bed for a few minutes thinking about the

implications of the murder, a government contractor being involved and wondered what was going on at those warehouses that was so important that they had to kill a man for finding an open door. He also wondered if his new friend–which he really wasn't yet, hadn't proven himself to be so, would be of any help to the Lakota people on this and other matters. It would be a good thing to have a county deputy in their pocket. He had an idea who this Phil guy was that Mike used to sweat with in California. If he was right there was a chance the wasicu could get an invite to go to lodge on the rez. He personally didn't sweat but Tully did, and was all into sweat lodge and Native American spirituality.

Hobart War Club was making plans as he fell asleep; the sound of his wife watching The Price is Right in the front room was the last thing he heard till his phone rang five hours later.

Mike showered and went over to grab a grilled cheese and fries in the VFW Post before going back to his Airstream to catch up on social media. He spent way too much time on his Chromebook these days: Facebook, Words with Friends, E-Mails and the like. A lot of the buddies back in SoCal wanted to know all about South Dakota and how he was doing as a Sergeant and a County Sheriff's Deputy. There were a lot of jibes back and forth, some calling him a traitor playfully … maybe not so much so: he couldn't tell. He didn't have a girlfriend and wasn't enrolled in an online Master's program yet so he justified his excessive media time this way.

He was just about to start getting dressed for work–he wanted to go in a little early and see how many reports and other items were in his in-box–when a County SUV pulled up outside next to his trailer. Max gave one sharp bark in warning and stood up. The high pitched yips of Mike's Cattle Dog always made him jump.

When Mike opened the door to see the county SUV, he knew two things: the driver was a sergeant like himself, and something was up.

A slender middle aged white man with a big bushy mustache got out with a cigarette in his mouth and walked up to Mike's little fence. Mike told Max to lay down in German, as all his official *this-means-business* commands were in German, and closed the door, stepping down to meet the approaching deputy.

"You Sergeant Taylor? One day on and already making waves," the man said with a note of annoyed sarcasm in his voice. He obviously wasn't a fan of having an outsider hired as a sergeant or his immediate connection to the red man.

"Yessir, I'm Taylor. Call me Mike. And you are?" Mike asked, trying to make a friend with his smile as he offered his hand. He'd been taught from a young age to make your smile and your handshake your best friend.

The sergeant shook it, reluctantly.

"Get dressed. Your *presence* has been requested … at Tribal Headquarters no less! Lieutenant Hicks says you are approved to go, in *civilian clothes*, and in your own vehicle. He will cover roll call for you. Something about that body dumped over the fence yesterday. Report to Hicks directly when you get to the station. We don't work cases with the Tribals normally, just so you know. I know you're new here and I heard you are Army; so am I, so I'll give you the benefit of the doubt, but a lot of people are watching you, *Sergeant.*"

"Well I appreciate that Sergeant, I really do. I'm just trying to win hearts and minds here, you know the drill. I'm a cop first," Mike said.

"Glad to hear it. My name is Heck, Jimmy Heck, 101st Airborne. Nice to meet you. Sorry about the circs," he said, using the abbreviated term for circumstances and shook Mike's hand again before leaving.

Mike went back in and got dressed quickly, rolling up his uniform and gunbelt and stuffing them in his gym bag. He gave Max a pat on the head and headed out for Tribal HQ. It was about a thirty minute drive. He noticed a lot of L & M Logistics trucks on the road going the other direction, two of them full eighteen-wheelers rather than the normal single box truck he had been seeing.

When Mike walked into Tribal Police Headquarters, he was already pleasantly impressed. Everything looked, for lack of a better word, *normal.* It was a nice well lit office building, one story with police cars out front, and even the roads leading into this government area were paved all the way in. He was getting a lot of looks from the secretarial and front desk staff, but he was used to that.

"Can I help you?" asked a female Tribal Police Officer, working the front desk.

"Yes, I'm Sergeant Taylor from the Pine County Sheriff's Department. I was called over?"

"Right. I'll call back there, Takoda said someone was coming from 'county', " she said and picked up the phone to call the back offices. "Yea, that guy's here from county."

She hung up and went back to the paperback book she had been reading when Mike came in.

Takoda, Mike thought to himself. That word was familiar but he couldn't quite place it. He spoke Lakota but wasn't born into it. A lot of words can have several meanings depending on how they are used in a sentence. For the most part, he was thinking Takoda meant very friendly or friends with everyone, but he wasn't sure. Since it was being used as a name he figured it meant a friendly guy.

A door opened to the rear of the front office area and Sergeant War Club stepped half-way out, dressed in civilian clothes like Mike save for a pair of cowboy boots and a western-cut button up shirt and Levi's with a big silver belt buckle. It was quite the contrast: The white man wearing Wrangler jeans, a Boba Fett T-shirt and an Army baseball hat and an American Indian dressed like a cowboy. *To each his own*, Mike thought as Hobby motioned him to come back. Mike looked for a way in and saw a little half-gate off to the right of where the front desk was and walked over and pushed through. It was not locked. The desk officer didn't look up from her book but a few of the secretaries in the office did.

"I hope you got more sleep than I did!" Hobby said as Mike walked up to him.

"Yeah, why?"

"We kinda did what you wanted us not to do. We tend to do that when the white man tells us not to do something," he said, smiling.

"Good. I was wondering about that all night. I wasn't too impressed with the sluggo the department sent out to investigate … that's between you and me. What'd you find out?" he asked.

"Come on: I want you to meet someone first, then we'll tell you all about it."

Hobby turned and held the door for Mike to catch as he went inside the inner offices of the Tribal Police Headquarters. It looked like similar bullpens back home. This was the investigators' offices. Mike saw a man sitting at a desk smiling his way as they approached and noticed Tully, also in civilian clothes–a black thin windbreaker and jeans—with his feet propped up on a desk in a far corner, apparently sound asleep.

"What's up with Tully?" he asked.

"Didn't get much sleep," Hobby said, coming up to the investigator, still smiling at him as he approached.

The man stood up and Mike noted that although short, about five foot two inches tall, he was dressed like the typical police investigator: slacks with dress shoes and a sport coat, button up shirt but no tie.

"Hi Sergeant, I've heard a lot about you. My name is Seth Armandarez, but my people call me Takoda," the man said, smiling even broader and sticking out his hand even before Mike could.

When they shook he noted how firm and genuine the handshake was. It complemented the man's smile. *So Takoda must mean friend to everyone,* he surmised afterall.

"Have a seat, have a seat. Sorry for the mess," Takoda said, "Hobby, why don't you tell him what you did first, so we can stay in chronological order. I like it when things are presented to me in chronological order, it keeps me from getting confused."

Another door opened and a big older Native American man came in wearing a Tribal Police Uniform with Lieutenant's bars on his collar. He looked to be in his fifties.

"Lieutenant Running Bear, do you want to sit in on this?" Takoda asked, still smiling with that disarming smile.

"Yup, I want to see this Deputy that speaks Lakota," he

said with curiosity as he took a sip from an Oglala Lakota College coffee cup and walked over.

"Okay," Sergeant War Club began, being more official now that the brass was listening, "We called you here because I have a liaison with you on this case, which as it turns out is our case, and we wanted to present this information to you to take forward to your superiors in the hopes that they will turn it over to us or at least work it as a joint investigation.

"After we left you we went to the man's house for a few reasons: first, you told us not to," he smiled before continuing, "John LaVoy was Lakota and his relatives deserved to know that he was killed. Turned out he had a wife. We, Tully and me, had the sad duty to tell her. She pretty much fainted right there on the spot. It was a sad scene. We learned he was a security guard at the L & M Logistics double warehouse on the rez. They're a government contractor that supplies all sorts of electronics to the rez. At any rate, he was on the phone with his wife last night and said he found an open door, it was late, and he had to call his supervisor. That was the last she heard from her husband. She did say that he was not supposed to go inside the warehouse. When he didn't call back she got worried, even more so when his supervisor called about an hour later asking if he was at home because he wasn't at work. She waited till morning time and reported him missing, calling into the front desk. We have the report. He's an adult so it's just a one-pager, check-the-box type report. You know the kind. I then called Takoda and his partner, David Swallows. I went home until I was called back in this morning. Tully stayed a bit later.

"Takoda, do you want to pick it up from there?" War Club finished, handing it over to the investigator.

"Absolutely," Takoda said, still smiling. It looked like this smile was a permanent fixture on the man's face, not forced at all–natural. "We called the supervisor, getting the number from Helen LaVoy (that's the decedent's wife) and he told us that when he arrived LaVoy was gone, the place was locked up tight, but a truck was missing and a dock was wet as if it had just been hosed off. I'm going to get a warrant to go check the business but since it's a government contractor there's a lot of red tape. No one is answering inside and the supervisor is just security and only has responsibility for the yard. We towed LaVoy's car that was still at the scene. It's obvious this is where the murder occurred. What we don't know is why: was it a foiled robbery, or did LaVoy see something he wasn't supposed to see? Oh, one more thing, was there a cellphone on his person, do you know?"

"Not that I know of. To be honest it was just a scoop and run out there after you and Tully left," Mike said, looking to Hobby briefly, before turning his attention back to Takoda, "he was just photographed and the coroner's people lifted him onto a body bag for transport and took him in. The investigator wasn't too gung-ho. I will follow up when I leave here."

"Chubby guy with a greasy comb over?" Takoda asked.

"Yea, that's him," Mike said.

"Barton. I've had dealings with him before. If the victim is Lakota he won't move too fast; probably doesn't even have a name yet. Back to the cellphone. We'd like to see that phone and will pull records for any calls or location pings if we can. My partner is out at a diesel repair place down the street. It's a long shot but they have cameras. Not good ones– the cheap Chinese tool warehouse kind–but it should show the only road leading back to the warehouse and we could get lucky with comings and goings, times, et cetera. That box truck had to come out on its way to dump the body. The cameras inside and outside L & M will be on the warrant too," Takoda said before continuing, "We'd like you to present the case that we're working. We'd like to solve this. Someone is trying to dump it off on the county, slow things down."

"Well, I'm supposed to call my lieutenant as soon as I leave here; he's taking roll call for me right now. As far as what I can do, I don't know. I'm just a street cop, deputy, whatever. I'll present it–I'm pretty sure you have more than we do–but I'm the new guy, so I don't know how much influence I have... yet." Mike said.

"That's right: you're new!" Takoda said, leaning forward and speaking with a bit more intensity now, "You speak Lakota and people are already talking about you…"

"KTALK Rez Radio!" came Tully's booming voice from across the room.

They all looked over at Tully who still had his head down, still looked like he was sleeping.

"Yes, you were mentioned on rez radio this morning by a caller. She thought it was cute that you speak Lakota. I think she works at the Thunderbird. So any help you can give us would be appreciated: this is our case and our people expect us to solve this case, bring justice in the end. This is going to get ugly: the white man is going to be blamed, the white race villainized in the death of this Indian. And so it goes on and on on this reservation. But if, just if, you can get through to them, your Sheriff may see the wisdom in working this joint. For race relations if nothing else." Takoda finished, looking at Mike hopefully.

"Something is fishy here," Hobby said, throwing in his two cents.

"Okay then," Mike said, after an uncomfortable silence, "I'll go see what I can do."

He got up and shook everyone's hands, with the exception of Tully, who still looked to be sleeping, although Mike doubted it very much. Probably just listening and resting his eyes.

Mike went out to his Tahoe, took a deep breath, opened the door, and got in. He waited till he was clear of Tribal Police HQ and off the rez before calling in.

Day Two

Mike's phone call to Lt. Hicks was brief: the Tribal Police were all over this investigation, the man was Lakota and had been dumped after going missing at work, notifications had been made and there were surveillance tapes involved along with a government contractor. Hicks told him he would have Detective Barton in his office when Mike got to work.

What Lieutenant Hicks did not share with Mike was that his second phone call this afternoon was upstairs.

A little while after Mike left Tribal Police Headquarters three things happened: first, Officer Tulliver Kangee Brown went home to bed (he'd taken the day off but said he would go out snooping tonight at the warehouses, *scout style,* or tomorrow night, after allowing things to return to normal*)*; Second, Sergeant Hobart War Club got dressed for work; third, Tribal Police Investigator David Swallows came in from pulling tapes from the diesel repair yard near the warehouses.

"You've got to see this!" he said excitedly to his partner.

"What have you got?" Takoda asked, looking up from the federal warrant application he'd just finished filling out, an AT&T phone records request copy also on his desk among other things. He'd sent that electronically a few minutes ago.

"I want to go back out, get all the comings and goings for the whole day, before and after the shooting, but I got it!"

David took out his cell phone, a big oversized "Phablet" job, and keyed up a grainy video he filmed from his phone while looking at a monitor screen at the business so the quality wasn't that great, a bit shaky too.

"What am I looking at, Dave?" Takoda asked.

"This is looking at the warehouse from the diesel repair on the corner, it's on their back yard area, corner of the building. See the warehouses there in the distance? I know, it's grainy, crappy cameras, 720p old school, but it's dark, right? This is about a half an hour after LaVoy called his wife, assuming the time stamp is accurate…"

"But I can't see anybody, or much of anything," Takoda said.

"Just watch!"

David pushed play on his phone and for a few seconds nothing happened. Then, there was a flash of light coming from the front area of the warehouse, just out of view.

"Oh!" Takoda said.

"Keep watching," David said.

A few seconds later there was another flash.

"So, two gunshots from outside the warehouse," Takoda concluded.

"*Exactamundo*! But wait: there's more."

David pulled up another little video clip on his phone and pushed play.

"This is like ten minutes later, about five minutes before the security supervisor arrives–I got that too," David said.

The second video clip showed a man pushing open the front gate as a box truck drove out and stopped. He then closed and locked the gate–not something a thief would be expected to do if caught in the middle of a burglary then killing the security guard and fleeing in haste. He then got in the passenger side of the truck and it left, driving right past the back of the diesel repair. "L & M Logistics" could be clearly seen–as clear as a grainy video of a video would allow–on the side of the truck as it went by.

"That's good work, partner," Takoda said, looking up at David, "What else did you get?"

"I saw the supervisor arriving and then another car a whole lot later, probably L & M people, and then workers started arriving for the day shift. I want to get everything! And the day before too. Two men were in the warehouse. Why? Right? What the fuck is going on there? But I need to take my laptop to make direct copies from the DVR system that runs those cameras. It's all stone-age shit. I'm heading back out. Where are we at–oh, and what happened with that Deputy?"

"He's cool. He's onboard, trying to get us the investigation but probably joint. I'm submitting the warrant to the federal judge now and the request for phone records is in. I'll keep you posted."

"Who's the Sheriff's Department detective on this?" David asked.

"Barton," Takoda said with disdain.

"Agh!" David said in agreement.

Detective Lou Barton was not a happy camper, sitting in a chair in the Watch Commander's office, waiting on the new sergeant to return from a meeting with the Lakota Tribal Police.

"Well, what the fuck do they want?" Barton asked before Mike could even take a seat.

"Nice to see you again too," Mike said in a defensive response.

"Lou," Lieutenant Hicks said, interrupting the exchange on purpose, "Sergeant Taylor may be new, but he's still a sergeant with a lot of training and experience. You will maintain proper decorum when speaking to him. He's made liaison with the Tribal Police and that is to our advantage. You got that?"

"Sorry LT," he said before turning back to Mike, "Sorry Sergeant, not used to sharing my case info with the tribals, they handle Indian stuff."

"Well, no offense taken, this *is* Native stuff. The man killed was Lakota. He was at work as a security guard at L & M Logistics, a government contractor on the rez, when he went missing. He had just called in an open door to the warehouse, but when his supervisor arrived LaVoy was gone along with a truck. He was obviously shot on the rez and dumped over the fence to throw things off. The question is *why*, and what's going on at that warehouse? His wife has been notified by the way, and more info coming—warrants, et cetera. Was there a phone on his body? The Tribal Investigators really want to know and check it. They are doing a ping request now. Bottom line is, this is their case but at the very least they would like to work it as a joint investigation with our department," Mike finished with a hopeful tone in his voice.

"No way," Barton said, frustrated, without even pausing to consider everything he was just told, he continued, "this is ours. I'll call them but that's it. How'd they even know his name? They checked his wallet before we arrived, that's how. I'm waiting on the autopsy, going over to get the belongings now. I'll let you know on the cellphone."

"Here's the Tribal Police Investigator's card," Mike said, handing him the card, "Call him. I've got to get dressed and get out there: my troops need me."

Barton took the card and left, obviously still perturbed by the situation.

Hicks smiled at Mike.

"That went well," Mike said, returning the Lieutenant's smile.

"Lots of people are looking at you Mike. Lots of people upstairs too. I'll make a call. Lou's a good ole' boy. He's gonna hate you!" Hicks said, smiling even broader.

Mike left and went to change shirts quickly before grabbing his unit and going in service. He stopped by the report room to check his box first. It was completely full. This was the part of becoming a supervisor that he wasn't looking forward to: reading reports. He stuffed the stack of papers into his gym bag and headed to the locker room just to change; he didn't even have a locker. He was hoping to do some more exploring of the area today but now he would have to park it somewhere and go over reports. From the look of the stack, there were various types of reports along with citations. This would take hours.

When he made it out to the Sergeant's SUV, he found a familiar looking pink donut box on the passenger seat with a note sticking out of it. The note was written on a pocket sized piece of notepad paper. It read…

Have a Donut Kid!
Heck

He smiled. He wasn't on any diet currently, so he ate it. It was a little stale, probably from this morning but it was a donut, a copper's best friend. He'd yet to discover where the local donut shop was. From New York to California some things never changed and one of those was that cops loved donuts. Memories from his earliest days in law enforcement came flooding back. He remembered his first training officers using the local donut shops–each district had their preferred ones, often referred to on the radio by their nicknames (12 South – 1200 South Bristol Street, 3 East – 300 East 17th Street...etc.) – as locations to stop, grab a cup of coffee and make some teaching point, go over reports or just sit and tell war stories of the good old days.

One thing the Sheriff's department didn't have out here was a substation. He decided his Airstream made a great substation, so he headed over to the VFW to sit at his kitchen table and go over all those reports still stuffed in his gym bag. At least he had a basecamp along with his faithful dog to keep him company.

It didn't take him as long as he thought it would to go through everything. He noticed who his good report writers were and who his ticket writers were. He'd be making a roll call speech about calling in stops and officer safety again before calling out specific deputies for not following his guidelines, wanting to give them every opportunity to comply. He already knew what leadership style he wanted to have based in part on the supervisors he'd liked and disliked from Santa Ana. There was one Mustang lieutenant he'd had in the military that he'd really admired. That prior enlisted lieutenant was very cool: he stressed the four P's of leadership, those being Praise Publicly and Punish Privately, and he never wrote anyone up. No Courts Marshalls, no Commanders Nonjudicial Punishment, also referred to as an Article 15. He would just have a senior sergeant take the offender for a "walk in the woods," so to speak, not coming back until the soldier's attitude was properly adjusted. Mike knew he wouldn't get away with that in a civilian setting, but still he admired it.

He looked at his watch and stuffed the reports back into his bag. It was time to eat.

Sergeant War Club was already in the last booth at The Thunderbird when he arrived, as were two plain clothes officers. Mike recognized one as Takoda, but he didn't know the other, probably the partner he'd yet to meet.

"Hello again Sergeant," Takoda said, "This is my partner David Swallows. He's got some interesting developments to share with you. How'd it go with Barton?"

Hobby slid over, giving Mike the preferred outside edge of the table, perhaps knowing the deputy would feel very boxed in if he'd gotten out of the booth and made

Mike slide in against the wall, completely trapped and at the mercy of the three Tribal Policemen and the elements.

"About as we'd expected it to go. 'No way,' being about the gist of it. But my lieutenant said he was going to make a call upstairs so stand by to stand by, right? And, nice to meet you David. Can I call you Dave?"

"Yea fine, just don't call me late for dinner," Dave said jokingly.

Hobby decided they were all having burgers, declaring it was his burger day, and they ordered before Dave once again took out his big phone and repeated what he'd already done twice, showing first his partner and then War Club, the two clips he'd taken earlier in the day. Mike watched the first clip, looking up at the investigators after the first flash. Dave tapped the top of his phone with emphasis, signaling there was more to see.

"He was shot twice," Mike said.

Then the second clip rolled and he saw there were two men.

"You know I've been seeing a lot of L & M trucks rolling in," Mike added.

"They're probably emptying the place as we speak!" Hobby interjected.

"Nothing we can do about that," Takoda said, "I'll have the warrant tomorrow for a search and the surveillance tapes from the L & M warehouse–if they haven't been wiped, which I suspect they will be. The manager of that place wouldn't even talk to me today, referring me to the company lawyer!"

"So, what's your next move?" Mike asked.

"We wait to see if the rest of the video reveals anything else for the day before and after and when and if your department decides to play ball with us. Oh, and Tully is going out on a little unauthorized surveillance tonight or tomorrow night." Takoda finished.

"We have our ways," Hobby added, making a sinister face and steepling his fingers together like a villain in an old horror movie.

Half way through their burgers Mike's phone rang and he answered it, listened mostly and said yes sir twice before hanging up.

He looked at the three Tribal Policemen and smiled.

"Well white man, you gonna tell us or what?" Hobby said, acting more perturbed than he really was.

"We have a joint investigation," Mike said and picked up his half eaten burger, a satisfied smile on his face.

Day Three

Mike was getting into his new routine, although he knew that would change slightly on Tuesday when he planned on moving his Travel Trailer up to Captain Trask's property. Today was calisthenics and weightlifting day and he got at it early, right after his morning cup of coffee and internet surfing. He needed to find a girlfriend, he thought to himself. He finished his workout and went over to the lodge for some food, showered, and got off to work on time, telling Max he was in charge of the Airstream.

Roll call went well, one of the resident deputies even making it in to meet the new sergeant. Mike brought up two things that he wanted to put emphasis on. First he addressed the car stops, stressing again to call in all stops, even if it's for a warning, telling them that a simple car stop for something as little as a tail light out could turn into a shooting in a matter of seconds: there was no way of knowing what state of mind any particular driver is in when pulled over or what they may have just done. Secondly, he touched on report writing and the need to cover the Corpus Delicti of a crime in the narrative on any crime or arrest report. After seeing a few questioning faces he explained, what he thought they should have known, that every crime has elements, or Corpus Delicti in Latin, and every element of the crime must be present or there simply is not a crime, the District Attorney's Office won't pick it up. *Perhaps they had forgotten*, he reasoned to himself. It wasn't something people talked about much after the academy and in small departments or rural areas where there were simply not a ton of arrests, these minor though important points of Law Enforcement minutiae can be forgotten.

Everyone went in-service and all was well. Mike went exploring out near the entrance of the rez near the clinic when he heard Deputy Rivera call in a felony car stop just a few blocks away, up the same street. It was the stolen Buick from the rez. Dispatch announced emergency radio traffic only and Mike radioed he was enroute. Deputy Henry Martinez, one of the twins, also said he was enroute from the station. Mike put the gas pedal to the floor and he hit the lights and siren. He was back in the game now and it felt good, the engine thrumming with power and the siren wailing, the transmission winding up and shifting, the radio beeping every few seconds to tell deputies there was an incident in progress and not to key your radio to ask if you're clear to go have lunch or call in a non-emergency trivial matter.

Deputy Rivera was standing behind her open door, gun drawn, speaking on her PA when he pulled up. He had to pass her and do a U-turn. She had the occupants of the vehicle, four young Native American males, with their hands up inside the car. Mike pulled up to the left of her Crown Vic (Ford, Crown Victoria model police special) and cut his siren, leaving his lights on to stop traffic coming up from behind. He opened his own door and unholstered his Glock, pointing it at the center of the back window of the Buick.

He heard another siren coming and knew Martinez would park behind Rivera and come up on foot between vehicles, which he did as Rivera was telling the driver of the vehicle to drop the keys for the vehicle out the window onto the ground with his left hand. *She was good*, Mike thought. *Textbook*.

Mike lowered the passenger window of his SUV and told Martinez to be the cuffing officer, handing him his own handcuffs and hoping to himself that either Rivera or Martinez carried extra cuffs or they were going to be a set short. He had turned in his supply of big zip ties, referred to as Flex Cuffs, when he left Santa Ana as they were city property. He didn't think to ask for some when he started here.

Rivera had the driver get out first with his hands up. She told him to lift his shirt and rotate in a 360 degree circle so the deputies could see his waistband. She then had him place his hands behind his neck and interlace his fingers and slowly walk backwards towards her voice. Martinez walked forward from between the patrol vehicles where he grabbed the young man by his interlaced fingers and patted him down for weapons with his strong hand, retaining his grip on him with his off hand. He then cuffed one wrist and swung the man's arms down, one at a time, to the small of his back where he completed the handcuffing procedure. He then took the driver and placed him in the back seat of Rivera's vehicle.

This was the procedure. They would repeat this until all four were out and cuffed and placed in vehicles and then they would approach the stolen vehicle, guns drawn, to look for anyone hiding inside. They would then check the trunk and do a search of the vehicle for weapons and contraband before calling a tow truck and having it impounded.

However, after the driver was hooked up and they were about to start on the passenger, Rivera having him scoot over to exit the driver's side of the vehicle, Officer Tulliver Kangee Brown showed up.

Mike saw the Tribal Police SUV coming up the opposite side of the street, emergency lights on without siren and passing vehicles that had stopped for the emergency activity. Mike had no way of knowing it was Tully until his SUV passed the first vehicle stopped facing him in the oncoming lane, pulling his unit sideways across it to prevent anyone from attempting to sneak past the police activity. He got out of the SUV and walked forward, staying out of the line of fire to come around the Sheriff's Department vehicles and behind Martinez and Rivera.

"Hey, we got this chief!" Martinez said.

Mike couldn't believe Martinez just said that to a neighboring law enforcement agency stopping by to assist. Tully was a little out of his jurisdiction, but it was the right thing to do. He realized the distrust between the department and the Tribal Police really was bigger than he'd anticipated.

"Tully, you got Flex Cuffs?" Mike yelled out to defuse the situation and include Tully beyond the dismissal of his subordinate.

"I have a double cuff case Sergeant," Rivera shouted back over her shoulder, "We're good! Officer, can you cover the passenger side in case someone bolts?"

That was good, Mike thought. He wasn't sure if Rivera was just being competently tactical or if she picked up on his vibe to include the Tribal Officer.

Tully moved over to the passenger side of Rivera's Crown Vic and provided cover without a word. Mike was not happy with the Martinez twin's choice of words and would have to talk to him later about it.

Rivera continued removing all the occupants of the vehicle, Martinez cuffing them until two were in the back seat of Rivera's unit and two were in the back seat of his unit, all cuffed, all searched. Rivera and Martinez approached the vehicle to search for hidden occupants, guns still drawn until it was clear. Tully moved over to the curb to keep the approaching deputies out of his own line of fire in the event someone popped up and started shooting (which didn't happen). Tully didn't even draw his revolver. He just stood with one hand on his gunbutt.

"Clear!" Rivera announced, as she holstered her weapon.

Mike holstered his as he looked to traffic control. He noticed the cars behind him were still stopped with a few doing U-turns, not that all that many cars were stopped at this off hour. They could wait a few, he decided. It was about the same on the other side of the street behind Tully's sideways SUV. He walked over to the curb–where most officers ended up after a felony car stop to discuss what came next. Tully stepped up and met Mike a few feet before the curb.

"I know these boys, Sarge. The car is his aunties car. It's not really stolen. He takes it without permission from time to time is all. She won't actually press charges," he said.

"Bullshit, Sarge!" Rivera snapped, stepping forward, "This is my felony arrest!"

Mike was kind of between a rock and a hard place. He knew Tully was telling the truth, but he also had to do right by his deputies. This was a test of his loyalties and leadership.

"Frickin Tribal's always showing up to bail out their Indian pals," Martinez said, throwing in his own two cents.

Tully turned around and looked at Martinez with an icy stare.

"Martinez, call a hook and go shake the vehicle," Mike said, to get Martinez out of the way for a few minutes.

He moved off and Mike motioned Rivera to step closer. He then turned to Tully and winked at him with his right eye, which Rivera couldn't possibly see from her angle.

"This is what we're going to do. You process and book the driver for possession of a stolen vehicle–what happens after that isn't our concern. We'll get the horsepower on the other three and release them to Officer Brown here. He can take them back to the rez, do with them what he wants: they weren't the driver so not in possession of the vehicle. And, thanks for the assist Officer Brown. Want to stand by while Rivera and I FI (Field Interview) the three, get their names and horsepower, and then you can have them?"

"Works for me, Mike," Tully said.

Rivera cocked an eyebrow at the Tribal Policeman's use of his first name. She then moved to the back of Martinez's unit, opened the back door, and started asking those two their names, dates of birth and home addresses.

"Martinez, call a tow, would you? I'll get traffic moving," Mike said.

Tully gave Mike a nod of approval and walked over to his SUV, pulled it around to the back of the Sheriff's units next to the curb and took the emergency lights off of rotate, leaving on just the rear amber flashers. Traffic started moving on the opposite side of the street. Mike pulled his SUV forward past the Buick and did likewise with his lights. He then walked back and started directing traffic slowly past the vehicles now that there was room for them to pass in the center common left turn lane of the street.

After Rivera did records checks over her radio with dispatch, she was satisfied the three had given real names and had no warrants. They uncuffed the three passengers and Tully took them and headed back to the rez. Rivera left to process the driver and book him into county jail, leaving Mike at the scene with Martinez who was filling out the tow form, waiting on the tow truck. Mike walked up to the driver's window of his unit where Martinez sat writing so he could monitor approaching traffic and still talk to Martinez.

"What are you Martinez, Mexican or Spanish?" he asked.

"What does that matter?" Martinez said, sudden irritation in his voice.

"Well I was wondering, would you like me, or anyone else for that matter, to call you a *wetback* or a *conquistador? Beaner, taco bender,* would that be cool?"

"What the fuck!" Martinez was mad now, stopping his writing to glare up at his sergeant.

"That would piss you right the hell off, wouldn't it? Especially if I did it in front of your coworkers?" Mike said.

"What are you talking about, sergeant?" he asked, still very pissed off.

"Calling Officer Brown 'Chief' is not cool. I don't want to hear that shit again. Native Americans, which is what they preferred to be called, not 'Indians', look up to their Chiefs. A Chief is an elder, a person of reverence and a leader of his people. You put him down just like you wouldn't want to be put down with racial epithets. If you don't understand that maybe you need some sensitivity training. Racism is not cool, for anybody. He stopped to help. The Tribal Police are a neighboring agency that is all. Are you picking up what I'm putting down?" Mike finished.

"Yeah, I get it. Are you going to write me up?" Martinez asked, looking a bit sheepish now.

"Nope. This is between you and me," he said, tapping the roof of his unit.

Mike then walked up to his SUV and went back in service, driving away.

At what had now become the normal time, Mike headed over to the Thunderbird Cafe for dinner. He knew Hobby was off today so he planned on just sitting at the counter somewhere near the back of the room, not wanting to take up a table by himself. He was surprised to see Takoda sitting in the back booth with a big grin on his face as usual, motioning him to come back.

"Hay Takoda, didn't expect to see you here! What's up?"

Mike sat down letting Takoda watch his back. He was getting more comfortable with that. Takoda seemed a top notch investigator and perfectly capable of watching his 6 o'clock.

"I wanted to thank you for your help in getting the joint investigation although I think I've gotten as much as I'm going to get out of Barton for a while. He cataloged LaVoy's personal effects and handed them off to me to return to Mrs. LaVoy. No phone was found. Probably taken by the killers. The autopsy isn't finished yet but he verbally confirmed that LaVoy was shot first in the stomach. He probably dropped to his knees–we'll confirm with any knee bruising–and the killer delivered the coup de gras then. They loaded him up, hosed off the blood, and took off."

"What about additional footage on that crappy video system up the street?" Mike asked.

"Funny you ask. Dave is still going through it but he did get the day before's footage and a Black Chevy Camaro came in at 9 PM and did not leave. It has smoked windows so he couldn't tell if there were one or two occupants. But last night Kangee did a surveillance on the warehouse and saw the Camaro arrive with two occupants and park in the back. It was there all night. And trucks are definitely emptying that place out fast!" Takoda said.

"Who's Kangee? What is that, Crow?"

"That's Tully, what we call him and yes, it means crow. You do know a lot of Lakota, don't you?"

"I know a fair bit. I wouldn't call myself fluent. Are you going to eat?" Mike asked as a waitress arrived to take their order.

Mike could tell he was becoming a regular because he didn't get as many looks from the people when he came in as he used to.

"You bet, I'm starving!"

They ordered and began to talk more off the subject, especially as two women sat down in the booth just behind Mike. A little Lakota boy of about 5 began immediately looking over the seat at him. He looked over at the boy who ducked back down quickly out of shyness. Mike couldn't see the mother but from the conversation it appeared she was sitting with her own mom.

Their food arrived after a while and they began to eat. Mike was cutting his steak when he saw an eagle feather with a beaded lower quill and leather straps come over the seat into his view, held by the boy.

"Oh, an eagle feather," Mike said in Lakota, "Did you find it?"

Out of his peripheral vision he could see the boy shake his head indicating no. At the same time he heard the boy's mother whisper to her mother, "Is the wasicu policeman speaking Lakota?"

He didn't hear a response so he figured her mother probably nodded.

"Hi Benny. Was that your dad's eagle feather?" Takoda asked, with his disarming smile.

The boy nodded in the affirmative to this question.

"That's big medicine. Why do we honor the eagle feather?" Mike asked the boy softly over his shoulder.

"Because it makes us speak the truth," Benny said.

"That's close my friend, very close. It *inspires* us to speak the truth and to follow the Lakota way of life so we can all soar as high as the eagle," Mike said, keeping the explanation as short as possible for the child.

"Excuse me," the boy's mother said, turning in her seat, "Can you not teach my child *our ways?* I am his mother. I will teach him."

Mike was a bit embarrassed and taken aback. He really didn't mean any harm.

"Yes ma'am."

Takoda raised his eyebrows, still smiling. They went on eating in silence for a while.

He heard the older woman scold her daughter in a whisper, "He was not wrong Wichahpi, That was mean."

Wichahpi, which means star, was a common girls name in Lakota. Mike recognized that right away.

The two men finished eating and Takoda grabbed the check, saying it was his treat for assisting the Tribal Police in the investigation, thanking him again for advocating for a joint investigation. They got up to go pay at the front counter before leaving. Mike looked at the younger woman and her mother. Star was a beauty: that was for sure. The feather *was* Benny's father's. He wondered how the man died. It was a shame for such a beautiful woman of any race to be widowed with a child at her age. It must be very hard on her, he thought, smiling at Benny as he walked by.

Mike sneaked a peek back there as he turned from the front counter to walk out with Takoda. Star was watching him. She didn't appear angry anymore. She almost had a look of curiosity on her face. Benny waived at Mike again with his eagle feather.

"Wow! She bit my head off!" Mike said to Takoda as they walked to the back row of cars.

"She's from a traditional family. She's a really good dancer. You should come out to the intertribal Pow Wow this coming weekend and see her dance, listen to some drums. You like that, right?"

"I work weekends unfortunately, junior sergeant. How did the boy's father die?" he asked.

"Traffic accident a few years ago. She was a top dancer then, took a few years off the circuit. It's nice to see her dancing again. This weekend is a lead up to the big Pow Wow, to pick the best of our rez. Come on out before work, have some fry bread tacos or buffalo burgers! They start at like 10 AM; you have plenty of time to get to work. Kangee, or Tully as you know him, he'll be there: he's traditional. He always goes. I'll stop by too."

"I'll definitely consider it. Hey, thanks for lunch and keep me informed on this investigation. I guess I won't hear anything now that the big investigators are working it. Not counting on Barton to tell me anything: I don't think I'm on his Christmas Card list," Mike laughed.

"I will."

"The boy speaks pretty good Lakota too," Mike added.

"Mike, they teach it in the schools now, so our way doesn't die."

"Oh, I didn't know that." Mike said as they said good-bye and got into their vehicles.

Week One

Mike's Friday, which is really Monday to the rest of the civilian world, was relatively uneventful. No news on the investigation. This was probably the way it was going to be unless he called Takoda; he sure wasn't going to call Barton. He finished all the paperwork for the week, drove around, wrote a speeding ticket and stopped by a DUI (Driving Under the Influence) stop and watched his deputies conduct a field sobriety test for a few minutes before driving off. One of the deputies gave him a thumbs up, which Mike took to mean additional backup was not needed. Back home in Orange County, where Santa Ana was located, officers held up four fingers signaling Code-4, a radio code for no further assistance needed. Guess they didn't have the code-4 thing out here in South D.

He ate at the counter of the Thunderbird by himself today, the hostess making sure to refill his ice tea about ten times, smiling at him repeatedly. If the roles were reversed, him smiling at her all the time, that would be deemed creepy. Funny how that worked. She was a cute girl; nice, attractive face with raven black straight hair with an amazing sheen to it. She was just curvy like a lot of

Native American girls were. That's what happens when another race invades and occupies a country and interrupts the natural evolution and eating patterns of the indigenous peoples. It messes with many things, not just their diet, having long term health issues. When blacks were brought over from Africa it affected them in many ways still having medical complications over a hundred years later. He had studied this in college, Native American studies being one of his electives. He knew food, much like stories and traditions were passed down from generation to generation. With western expansion after the Louisiana purchase in 1803, many tribes were rounded up, relocated, their diets interrupted permanently. Things like lard, flour, sugar, coffee and canned spam meats led to weight gain, heart disease and diabetes.

Mike knew he was being shallow. She was pretty. So he decided she was too young for him. He justified things this way to himself and tried to dismiss the thoughts.

On the other hand, a Lakota girl like Star, widowed with a child would be no problem…

A few hours later there was an all call, asking any deputy in the area, to respond to an injury traffic accident out on State Route 6. A few units answered up saying they were enroute and Mike rolled that way as well. When he got there an old timer named Ahern already had things well in hand, flare pattern already laid, lit, and burning on the ground and the second deputy, Johnson, who was half

Lakota, was assisting Ahern with gathering info off the vehicles involved as Ahern talked to the occupants, one holding his wrist as if it was broken–probably from gripping the steering wheel tight as the airbag deployed…

Medics had been called for just before he arrived, so he parked off the roadway with his full rotating red lights on to slow down traffic well in advance on this state highway.

Both vehicles were off the roadway. One was in a ditch to one side and the other had spun around facing the opposite direction and came to rest half off the shoulder and onto the dirt. From the damage Mike could see walking up, the vehicles being a good hundred feet apart, it looked like this was a head-on sideswipe accident: someone had drifted slightly left of the center line for whatever reason–inattention, texting, or intoxication, he had yet to learn which. Ahern had the occupants off the roadway and in front of his unit, protecting them from oncoming traffic.

"We're good Sarge, hey, can you call me two tows? She hit her head on the side window and he definitely has a broken thumb from the airbags," Ahern said.

"You got it," Mike said, leaning his face over to the handheld radio mic clipped to his shirt's shoulder, "Pine 301, we'll need two tows please."

"Pine 301 copy, two tow trucks enroute," the dispatcher acknowledged.

Mike wondered just how many tow truck companies there were out here. In Santa Ana they had 6 or 7 companies in the rotation and it being only a 27-square-mile city, an officer was pretty much guaranteed a truck at his location within 15 minutes, rain or shine, day or night.

Ahern went to his trunk and retrieved a can of orange neon spray paint from what appeared to be a personal travel bag, and a walking tape measure on a wheel with a collapsible handle. He started walking towards one of the vehicles to mark where one of the tires came into contact with the pavement. Mike knew at that moment that Deputy Ahern was a traffic guy. He followed him out of earshot of the civilians.

"Isn't this a State Trooper case?" he asked.

"When they show up! I'll get it started," he said.

"Looks like you know what you're doing!" he commented.

"Accident investigation school like you," he said.

"I'll leave you to it then. Not going to micromanage," he said, turning and walking away.

"Greatly appreciated, California!" Ahern shouted over a passing vehicle.

Mike held his hand up in acknowledgement as he walked back to his SUV.

Funny how in law enforcement everyone found their niche. Ahern was a traffic guy. Some officers were into drugs and narcotics related arrests: paraphernalia, use and influence, and possession. Others liked traffic tickets. There was a big cult of officers that were really into stolen vehicles, another addicted to the graveyard shift. Indeed, many states, like California, had special awards for patrol officers that made multiple stolen vehicle arrests and recoveries, both rolling stolen vehicles and unoccupied stolen vehicle recoveries. Mike himself had four or five of these awards, called 10851 awards (the California Vehicle Code for stolen vehicles), given to him by the California Highway Patrol. He had yet to discern whether the South Dakota Highway patrol had such comparable awards. Finally, there were the sluggos, those officers who did nothing in terms of observation activity. These were the officers that for whatever reason, be it laziness or cowardice, didn't do anything and were used by dispatch for pending reports and food runs. And the crazy thing was, Mike knew, these sluggos were the most liked by both dispatch and supervisors. Why? Because they didn't get into any trouble, didn't crash any cars, didn't generate citizens complaints.

It was nice to know that Deputy Ahern could be counted on to do good traffic accident reports. He would count on him in the future when needed, not one of those officers, or deputies (he had to start thinking *deputy* and not *officer,* he told himself), that went into service and went straight to periscope depth until EOW (End of Watch).

Before EOW, Mike went to the county yard and gassed up the SUV and ran it through the little car wash there for Sergeant Heck. He liked that old veteran. And right now, Mike needed some allies in the department. After one week he had alienated at least two deputies and maybe, just maybe, he'd made a few friends…

Earlier that day, much earlier, at about half past midnight on what would be Mike's Friday, Officer Tully Kangee Brown parked his Jeep a few blocks away from the L & M warehouses and walked in on foot. Dressed in a camo hunting jacket and jeans, he walked slowly across a large field to the north side of the building where the murder occurred. He listened between each step as if he was back on patrol in the military. He knew that LaVoy had been replaced so there was at least one outside security guard, just for show more or less and Native American, to watch the outside of the premises. He also knew there were at least two real professionals on the inside, probably not Native American at all–part of the L & M organization or outside pros. Regardless of which, he did not want to be detected.

All was quiet as he crept closer. The box trucks were more visible through the 10 foot chain link fence and, as they suspected, there was the Black Camaro on the far side in the corner, backed into a parking space, not visible to the front of the building. LaVoy may have walked the lot. He probably did hourly when not snoozing in his car… He'd probably known of this car and who owned it. But he was dead now and there was no way to ask him.

Tully got right up to the fence, not seeing any outfacing cameras or sensors of any kind. Like a good soldier sent out on reconnaissance patrol, he got close enough to touch the enemy vehicles, count them, and if there had been enemy soldiers sleeping on the ground or in tents, counting coup (touching your enemy) on them too if needed. He took out a notepad and wrote down the license plate number of the Camaro. Then he backed up a good 50 yards, slowly, and walked around the entire property, slowly and deliberately, taking over an hour. He got what he came for.

Mike woke with a start, the sound of AK-47 automatic rifle fire fading in his mind. His hand had shot up to his chest, checking for his M-16 rifle that he slept with while on active duty, usually lying across his upper body. But it had just been a dream. He wasn't in the sandbox fighting Muslims for his country anymore. The Middle East was far far away now. The shootings, the violent incidents, and the blood of Santa Ana were far away now too, but thanks to a little thing called Post Traumatic Stress Disorder, the memories were not. PTSD was the gift that kept on giving. Studies have shown that law enforcement officers, much like soldiers in war, also develop PTSD over time, depending on the activity level of their agency.

He shook it off, got up and fed Max, and started heating

up the coffee maker. It was the first day of his RDO's (Regular Days Off) and he had things to do. It was time to pull up stakes, so to speak, and move the Airstream up the road. He wanted to go say goodbye to the VFW morning crew, hook up and go to the local RV campground and pay the dumping fee, dump his graywater and refuse tanks, fill up on water, and head out. Captain Trask's property was less than thirty minutes away so that was good, coming in handy for return trips to the RV camp to dump and fill. He figured if he used the showers in the department locker room he could stretch out the need to dump tanks.

Mike was on the road in thirty minutes, thinking of where the investigation was going. He would have to call Takoda. He couldn't wait to see War Club on his Monday. It was killing him.

Mike made it to the property just fine, up a final dirt road till he came to the front of Trask's house. The Captain's wife was in the front kitchen window looking out at him as he came to a stop, road dust drifting past him. He waved to her and she returned it, then pointed to the driveway just past the house. He could see the dirt driveway just past the concrete driveway in front of the garage. This led to the back of the property through an opened gate. He headed through slowly and saw a stand of trees in the distance that he and the good captain had discussed as a good flat area with ample shade, not too close to the old homestead, giving him space and distance. He drove slowly over the unimproved terrain and made a large arc, bringing his trailer up next to the trees, facing back out the way he had come in for easy egress on dump days. He didn't know how long he would stay here but it was a very pretty spot, a hill in the distance and a lovely area between trees for his propane fire pit and camp chairs. He could see himself spending many evenings out there...until it started to snow. That would be a whole different story, and something he wasn't used to.

But for now, this was home.

He spent the better part of the morning and early afternoon setting up camp, leveling his trailer, setting up his front porch and placing his propane fire ring out next to the trees with his four camp chairs. He told himself four chairs looked inviting. Putting out just one chair may send the message that he didn't want visitors, which was not true. Finally, he went in and fed Max and opened a can of chili for himself, frying up a few eggs and throwing them on top for good measure.

Mike was sitting out at his unlit fire pit eating when he saw Captain Trask coming up the dirt road in his truck. He parked in his driveway and went inside. After a few minutes the good captain walked out of his rear sliding glass door and waved to Mike, then went back inside. He emerged a few minutes later and began walking towards Mike's camp with something in his hand. As he got closer Mike could tell it was a cocktail, bourbon on ice he guessed.

"This is a great spot, huh? I don't know why I haven't

put a deck or gazebo out here?" he said as he got closer, "I love that fire pit! So, how are you doing?"

"Good! I'll have to pick up another heavy duty extension cord. I only have a two hundred footer," Mike answered.

"Don't worry about it, we'll figure it out," the Captain said, dismissing it with a wave of his hand as he took a seat opposite Mike. "You know, there's an old meter just over there," he said, pointing towards the fence line. "The guy that bought that parcel passed and his family has done nothing with that place. I bet you can call SD power and they can come out and hook you up."

"Have you heard anything on the joint murder investigation?" Mike asked, not able to contain himself or his curiosity any longer.

"Oh, Barton is hating it, but it was the right call. He went out today and accompanied the TP on their warrant for the warehouse. He said the cameras were wiped and they were generally uncooperative and the place was almost empty, just a few computers for the tribal schools and a few coin op washing machines. Definitely hiding something."

"Any blood?" he asked.

"Oh yeah, there were minute trace amounts on a dock area that showed up under UV light, whole dock smelled like bleach! Definitely some type of corruption going on, lot of that lately. FBI has been looking into the tribal government for years. Kick-backs on contracts for everything from construction to inside job placement, cronyism and the like."

"Was there any mention of a Black Camaro?" Mike asked.

"No, no Camaro was mentioned. Why?"

"Oh, I thought there was something about a Camaro," Mike said, instantly regretting saying it. Maybe that little fact was being held in reserve by his tribal friends…

"So, what's the theory," Mike asked, quickly changing the subject.

Trask took a sip of his bourbon.

"They had something in there the vic wasn't supposed to see. They killed him for it. Call Barton–scratch that: call your friends on the TP. Barton isn't a fan of yours at the moment from what Lieutenant Hicks tells me," he chuckled, "Hicks says the Tribals have bent over backwards to include Barton, even bought him lunch, invited him to Tribal HQ, but he won't go."

"That's too bad," Mike said.

"You gotta understand Mike, before you came here we didn't do much with the TP. Indians out here are much closer to the ugly past than your Mission Indians in California. The Little Bighorn, the Wounded Knee Memorial where the good ole US Cavalry gunned down men, women and children a hundred years ago is not too far from where we're sitting. Deputy Johnson is the closest we have to a Lakota but he is only half through his mother and they don't live on the reservation. And it was worse when I was out on patrol! We have a long way to go, but you making friends like right away is a good sign. Hell, maybe we could have a first annual Sheriff's Department slash Tribal Police picnic in the near future!"

"That's a thought. I'll float that idea," Mike nodded.

"Let's catch these bad guys first!" Trask said.

The two men talked till dusk with Mike taking the Captain's glass in his Airstream twice and filling it with ice and Proper No. 12 Irish Whiskey, Mike's favorite, before lighting the fire ring. Trask said he'd better go back into the house before it got too dark to see because he was getting pretty toasted on the fine spirits. He told Mike to call him Frank when at home which eased Mike's fears greatly: at least he'd made a positive impression on a few of the higher ups. That was a good sign, he thought as he watched Frank walk back to his house.

"Well, what do ya know about that?" he said to Max, who looked up at his master.

The dog laid his head back down on his paws, watching the fire.

Mike decided next time he spoke to the good Captain he'd try his luck and ask him if he'd mind him building a sweat lodge further up in-between the trees…

The next morning Mike and Max took a jog around the property a few times, noting the old electrical box on the base of a pole and making a point to come back later and get the numbers off of it and call the electric company. They would probably have to come out and do a safety inspection before allowing him to tap into that line. He may need permission from the landowner too; he wasn't sure.

After showering and doing his internet surfing for the morning, commenting on friends' Facebook posts, Instagram photos, and Tweets, he made a bologna sandwich which Phil, his Lakota neighbor growing up, used to call *reservation round steak.* He then took Max outside to work on some of his K9 skills they'd been neglecting this week. In order for a dog, or a human for that matter, to stay sharp, they need constant training and reinforcement. Being a working breed dog, Max loved it, running full speed through the tall grass.

After a good half an hour of training with the dog, Mike noticed an old 1962 Tan Ford truck slowly coming up the dirt road towards Captain Trask's house. Trask had gone to work and his wife had left also, perhaps for the grocery store or a friend's house. So Mike naturally kept an eye on the beat-up old truck as it crept ever closer to the residence. It hesitated out front then stopped in front of the dirt driveway leading back to where he stood watching. The truck then turned onto the dirt road and crept towards him.

Mike walked closer to the Airstream and called Max to heel. He thought of going inside and getting his Glock, but as the truck came closer he saw first the flowing white hair of an older person, and then the face of an old Native

American man in his seventies. Not that an old Native couldn't shoot him, but he decided to smile and remain friendly. He had Max to command to attack if need be. He told the dog to *sit* in German.

The truck came to a slow stop next to him, window down; the old man, closer to eighty than seventy Mike thought, looked over at him.

"Hao, kola. You Mike, the deputy on the Red Road I been hearing about?" the man said with a slow-paced voice often heard from the older Native Amerians more accustomed to their own tongue than English.

Mike was taken completely off-guard. Who was talking about him and who told this man where to find him? And what possible reason did this elder have for coming all the way out here to seek him out? These questions and others flashed through his head before he answered.

"Uh, yessir?" he said, his mind still searching.

"Get in the truck, youngster. We need to go cut some willow boughs and build a lodge. You got tobacco?"

Mike was floored. He didn't know who this elder was or where he would take him in that old beat-up truck, but he recognized it as an opportunity.

"Yessir," he said and turned to go in his trailer and grab a can of Bugler tobacco. He always had a few cans of Bugler around for prayers and blessings: it was an important part of Lakota spirituality. He assumed the man meant regular commercial tobacco or cahnlee (chan-lee) in

Lakota. There were several words for tobacco and different types of tobacco used in spiritual rituals. He thought of slipping his Glock in its clip-on holster onto his belt but decided against it, instead grabbing his wallet and cellphone and going back out the door, a can of tobacco in hand.

"Max, you're in charge," he said to the dog, telling him basically he wasn't going.

Mike got in, not even knowing the man's name.

Inipi

J anet Sweetwater Carter lived well on the reservation. She was the purchasing agent for the entire Lakota, Dakota and Nakota Nations, including the school districts. She had a big house near the tribal offices in an area where many of the more affluent Native Americans lived, perhaps living a bit too well…

It was early in the morning as she sat at her kitchen table sipping coffee she'd made in an expensive coffee maker, the nice disposable pod type machines, out of good quality coffee cups, a whole matching set, wearing her favorite robe from a fancy department store no less. Her husband, who worked in research and development for the rez, was still asleep on their top of the line adjustable mattress.

Things couldn't be better, she thought as she went over figures on her high-end laptop computer while KTALK rez radio played the morning news in the background. She was so happy with herself, so engrossed in the monetary figures she was viewing, that she did not hear the man walking up slowly behind her, garrote clinched between both fists, military issue balaclava covering his face. He slipped it quickly over her head and cinched it tight around her neck, lifting her suddenly and violently off her chair. Instinctively, her hands shot to her neck but it was no use, no help. Shock overtook her as she struggled to breathe, to free herself. Her assassin was too strong. He held her as she struggled and slowly slid towards death. She wondered, stars and blackness filling her vision, *What did I do wrong?* She had followed all instructions to the letter. There was no extra money in her bank accounts: it was all electronically delivered to her numbered offshore account for a rainy day. If she could just talk to him, the man that had approached her, surely she could work this all out. This was her last illogical thought as she slipped into unconsciousness and then death.

The man held her even after she went limp. He was well trained in his craft, for the art of garotting was not what TV and the movies portrayed: it was not five seconds and off to the next scene, it took strength and time. Breathing had to stop, the heart had to stop, the brain had to die.

It took several minutes of holding her till his biceps were cramping, listening for any sign of her husband arousing from bed, his own heart pounding in his chest, until he finally let her slip back down into her chair. He loosed the wire from her neck and reached over, unplugged the power cord from the side of the laptop, closed it, and slipped it under his arm as he crept out of the residence, his deed done.

An American muscle car with a throaty exhaust was all that was heard speeding away that morning.

Mike sat quietly listening to the old truck go through its gears manually. There was a sweet sound to those old engines. It reminded him of when he was a kid–hunting dove and quail with his dad in their old International Scout. He always wanted one. The sound of the transmission, especially in reverse with that high-pitched winding out sound it made. Maybe someday…

The old man didn't say much and it was making Mike a bit nervous. He was starting to regret getting in this truck if the whole day it was going to be like this. He didn't know what to say to break the ice but he needed to try something.

"I don't have any knick knick, or I would have grabbed that too," he said.

He regretted it as soon as he said it. Too lame, he thought. He knew the man meant commercial tobacco, or chun le, (chan-lee) and not knick knick, which is a mixture of local plants and tree bark that varied depending on the tribe or even the individual user. Knick knick literally translated to *that which is mixed.* The man said tobacco, which is used as an offering mostly; some put it in their mixtures for smoking in the sacred pipe. Before the white man came and introduced the nicotine tobacco smoking plant, Native Americans of the region smoked cansasa, (chun-sha-sha) which was dried red willow bark, from the inner soft part of the bark. But then, well, the white man in his wisdom took away many spiritual things from the red man in his attempt to civilize them. And the practice of smoking the nicotine plant began. It has become one of many health problems still plaguing the Native American today.

Mike was overthinking it.

"Why would you have knick knick?" the old man said, looking over at him momentarily.

"I guess I wouldn't. I don't even have a chanupa," Mike answered, referring to the sacred pipe smoked at the inipi, more commonly known as sweat lodge.

Only the spiritual leader, the man that poured the water on the stones at inipi, was the holder of the sacred pipe.

They turned onto the hard top from the dirt roads and headed for the reservation. The driving got a bit faster and much smoother.

"Want some c'ank'alyapi? (chank-alleppey)," the man asked, motioning to the thermos on the seat lying between them.

C'ank'alyapi is the traditional Lakota tea made from plants found on the rez. It had been used for hundreds of years and was used for a number of ailments, or just to drink as a tea long before the white man introduced European coffees and teas and definitely before they built a Starbucks on every city corner.

"Sure, thank you," Mike said.

He had tasted it before. Phil often drank it on lodge days. Now they were getting somewhere, he thought.

"Better have some now before we get off the road again."

Mike took the old thermos and unscrewed the little plastic cup that covered the screw-in lid. He put it between his legs and then unscrewed the lid, pouring himself about a half a cup to be polite. He didn't want to fill up the cup. He screwed the lid back in and sat the thermos back in between them and took a sip of the native tea. It was bitter. He must have made a face because the old man chuckled.

"There's no canhanpi, (chan-apee) in there. I don't use sugar, it's bad for you," he said.

"I must admit," Mike smiled, "I've only had it with sugar. Phil, the Lakota spiritual leader that introduced me to the Red Road when I was a boy, used lots of sugar."

"Phil *Velardi,*" the old man scoffed, "He's probably fat now!"

"You know Phil?"

"Is he fat?"

"Yes. Yes, he's got a belly," Mike had to admit.

"I knew it! Yeah, I know him," the man said.

"Can I ask you how you know him?" Mike asked.

The old man looked over at Mike for several seconds until Mike got worried enough to look at the road to see where the truck was going on its own. The old man then looked back at the road.

"You can ask…" he said, not answering the question.

"What is your name, uncle?" Mike asked after a pause.

"Tom Funmaker, but uncle is good. You call me that."

"Ok uncle. Where are we going?"

"Willow boughs. We need to go get the boughs to build a new inipi at my place," he said.

Funmaker was frustrating to talk to. Like many of the older Native Americans, he was somewhat short on facts and details. Oh, they were up there...in his head. He just didn't expound upon these thoughts. Mike wanted to know where the willow boughs were, and where his place was.

He sipped some more tea, mostly to be polite. He was determined to finish at least the amount he had poured.

"What do you know about building the inipi?" Funmaker asked.

This was a positive shift in the conversation, Mike realized. Funmaker was asking questions now and speaking first. Now they were definitely getting somewhere, and not just down the road.

"Well, I helped make one when I was about thirteen with Phil…"

"Agh, don't say that name! It hurts my ears!" Funmaker interrupted.

Mike hesitated before going on, a spark of intrigue rolling around in his mind. Funmaker knows Phil and there was some animus there, some angst. There appeared to be some history between the two men, but Phil was a good twenty years younger than Funmaker so this would take some delicate digging. He'd have to start with War Club on his Monday at the Thunderbird Cafe. Or Tully, as he was traditional and most likely to go to lodge on a regular basis. Probably knew Tom Funmaker…

"I know you take the boughs–we had to get a permit in California; you probably don't need that on the rez–and then you build the lodge, eighteen boughs, setting in the ribs, offering tobacco in each little hole, praying before the ground is prepared and after you are done, setting in the doorway facing the east and the mound and the fire pit with the crescent moon ridge around it...Oh, and prayer ties! Lots and lots of prayer ties for the first time you light the fire and you pray over the old lodge ribs and burn them in a good way." Mike was going way too fast out of excitement he realized and tried to slow himself down, "I tended fire many times before I was allowed to go in with the adults."

"What about the grandfathers? The rocks? Where did you get those? How many do you need?"

"We went out to an old lava field near Twentynine Palms in California whenever we needed more lava rocks. You know how sometimes they crack or explode when the water is poured on them?" Mike offered.

"Mmm, what about Inipi? What do you know about that? Not just the four rounds and how hot it gets–everyone knows that," Funmaker asked.

"Well, everyone smudges off with some sage before coming into the grounds; we light the fire and smudge the lodge with sweetgrass and we smoke the chanupa so there will be truth and we will have a good lodge. Then everyone goes in and the fire tender sends in the bucket of water and when the spiritual leader asks for some rocks the fire tender sends them in one at a time on a shovel after brushing the dirt and ash off best he can. Then they pray, maybe sing a song and each round has a specific purpose and when the leader thinks that round is over he pours the water and calls for the flap to be opened up. I've seen lodges that last an hour and I've been to lodges that lasted three hours. It all depends."

"Mmm, metal shouldn't touch the rocks. Better to use antlers to move the stones. But why do we go to lodge?" he asked.

"Well, for a vision quest, but I've never had a vision. I always understood it's more to reset your spiritual center, get right with Tunkashila and to come out of the womb of mother earth afterwards, reborn. To be humble again." Mike said.

"That's good. I like you used Tunkashila. That's what I grew up with, but Wakan Tanka is used more now for god. Tunkashila means grandfather. I'm sure you know that. Gotta be all correct these days in our words for the young-sters generation. Who taught the People about Inipi?"

"White Buffalo Calf Woman came down and taught us. She taught us the four powers of the universe: fire, water, earth and the air. Our prayers draw on all four elements and they are represented in the lodge itself. The earth is in the mound we build outside the door where the chanupa rests while we are inside. The fire heats the rocks like the sun heats the earth. The water we pour on the stones is life and the air is all around us. We must breathe air to live. We remember air is in each word we speak so we remember to be humble with our words."

"Hmm, you have some knowledge. This man who taught you did a pretty good job. The universe is repre- sented in each aspect of the lodge, from the way we build the grounds to how we sit during lodge. I will teach you more. What does Inipi mean to you, personally?" he asked.

"My mom tried to get me to believe in God and Jesus Christ, took me to church when I was young and I guess I believe in God and Jesus and all that–the holy trinity is an interesting concept and all–but I never had what I would call a *religious experience* attending the white man's church. But the first time I went into the lodge, sitting there in my underwear, and they closed the flap and it was pitch dark...that had an impression on me. Then when the first red hot rock was brought in and then the rest of them and we prayed as it got hot, wow, there is nothing like it. And finally when the leader pours the water and I got hit with that intense heat and my skin was burning, all I could think of was don't run out, don't run out and I've seen grown Indians bolt out of there! Only my prayers kept me in there. The hotter it got, the harder I prayed till that flap was opened and that sweet cool air came rushing in. And that was just the first round! I didn't know how I would get through three more rounds! But I did. And when that flap was opened the final time and I came out of the womb of mother earth I *did* feel reborn, you know, fresh, all the junk and oil sweated out of me, and my mind was reset. It's been like that every time."

"Waste (Wash-te)" was all Funmaker said, the Lakota word for "good."

They rode in silence for a while.

"I apologize for saying *Indian.* I think I said Indian back there…?"

"What?" Funmaker asked.

"Indian. I said Indian instead of Native American back there," Mike said.

This got a chuckle out of Funmaker.

"Do you know what we called ourselves before the grammar police came around, telling us to say *Native American* or *First Nations?* We said Indian. Injun, Indun, it's all the same. So it doesn't bother me. In Lakota we call ourselves *friend.*"

The two men spent the rest of the day building the lodge.

They traveled to the rez to a valley with a stream where many willows grew. More than enough willow boughs were harvested, tied together and placed in the back of the pick up. Funmaker had brought an extra old pair of ripped leather work gloves for Mike and they worked together, but mostly it was Funmaker directing and instructing Mike. Tobacco was offered and prayers were said to the four directions more than once. It was very familiar to Mike Taylor. Very familiar indeed.

Funmaker lived way out past the rest of the reservation populace. They traveled a long time, down bumpy roads, through dry washes, passing many old houses and trailers, most of them abandoned, until finally they went up a little rise after a wash to a naturally hollowed out area next to a hill. It offered good protection from the wind. It was here they found a single wide trailer with a water tank off to one side and a junkyard of old Ford trucks. There were perhaps twenty five of them, all around the same year, parked in various states of disrepair. Mike knew instinctively that Tom Funmaker liked to be alone–odd for a holy man–and that he scavenged old trucks to keep the one they were riding in going.

Then Mike saw the old inipi grounds off to one side. The wooden ribs were broken and it leaned almost on its side in a horrible state. The mound had weeds growing on it as did the old fire pit. It was obvious there had been no fires lit here for many many years.

Funmaker announced that he was hungry and would go make them some peanut butter and jelly sandwiches. He teased Mike with more c'ank'alyapi but laughed and said he had regular ice tea, no sugar. As he went into the trailer to make them, Mike walked over to the old grounds. It was even worse looking up close. He saw an old stack of blankets that looked like they had become one with the earth. He bent down and tried to lift one but it simply came apart in his fingers. It had been more than years–it had been decades. He spied a pile of tarps next to a shed and walked over to inspect those. They were rotted out too. They would need all new blankets and tarps for this lodge if they were going to sweat any time soon. In olden times actual animal hides were used to cover the lodge. Those days were long gone...

Mike stood and looked at the pile of igneous rocks in the old fire pit. They had been there too, all this time, however long it had been since the last time they had been lit. They were dirty. Rain had set the lower rocks into the ground and they were covered with dirt from years of rain hitting the ground, splashing mud up onto the pile. It was discolored with dirt half way up all sides. Most of this would burn off, fall into the ash when or if the fire were lit again. It didn't seem possible the way they looked now, the way it all looked now.

Funmaker came out with two sandwiches on one plate and two big cups of iced tea. He handed the whole plate to Mike followed by one of the large plastic cups. Then he reached over and grabbed one of the sandwiches off the plate and began eating, looking at the dilapidated sweat lodge grounds.

"There's a hula hoe in the shed there, watch out for snakes," he said between bites, "I'll move the ribs."

Mike finished his food and stood drinking his tea.

"The blankets and tarps are rotted out. We are going to need new ones. Is there a second hand store on the rez? Though I wouldn't want to take all the blankets…" Mike mused.

"What's this *we, white man?*" Funkaker said and then started laughing hard till he started coughing.

Mike didn't think it was that funny…

"I always wanted to say that!" Funmaker said, catching his breath, "Don't worry about the blankets and tarps. I have a connection. You just come back next Wednesday for a sweat, I have some more work to do to get this ready. I want to invite a few more people too."

The old man took Mike's cup when he finished and went back inside the trailer for a few minutes. Mike found the old hula hoe in the shed, covered with spider webs, brushed it off and set to clearing the lodge area of weeds. Funmaker came out and started to move the old ribs off to the side, breaking some in the process which set him to muttering under his breath in Lakota.

Finally they built the new lodge. Tobacco was offered and like he had done before many years ago, Mike set in the boughs after stripping them, while Funmaker watched, giving him instruction as needed. When a bough would creak and threaten to break under protest of the bending, Mike would stop and gently talk to the bough. And every time, it did not break. Funmaker nodded his approval every time till all the ribs were in, the cross ribs set and tied in and the doorway was fashioned. Then the lodge was done.

It was late afternoon when Funmaker drove Mike back to Captain Trask's property and his Airstream. They rode mostly in silence, thinking of the day and the lodge days to come. Mike couldn't help but wonder why this man had come to get him and why he had chosen to sweat again after what was obviously such a long time. There were many unanswered questions for Mike but he would not ask Funmaker anything further on the matter. He would investigate this one on his own. His thoughts wandered from the old days of sweating when he was a kid to now, the familiarity between how Phil had built a lodge and how Funmaker had him build this lodge...

It was probably just his imagination. After all, a protestant church and a catholic church both had pews and crosses in them. It must be the same with one Lakota lodge to another.

Funmaker chuckled a time or two to himself, still finding it funny about the white man comment he had made.

Mike didn't mind the joke one bit. He had grown up around negative comments about his race, some in jest and some not so much so, all his life. He chose this path of the Red Road not being a red man. But one thing stood out today and that was that both he and Funmaker said *we,* more than once. We will build… We need… We…

Twilight was just setting in when the old pickup pulled into the property and drove slowly towards his own trailer. Captain Trask and his wife were sitting at his fire pit when they pulled up, Max getting up and running over to meet them.

"Next Wednesday, uncle," he said as he got out.

Funmaker nodded and slowly drove off the property.

What is Known and Unknown

In dealing with PTSD, the shrinks at the VA say that following patterns, or having a *routine,* are important to mental health. Mike always tried to do things at the same time and that included having one day a week to relax. It was usually on whatever day his Sunday fell and today was the day. He slept in, didn't get dressed, stayed in his PJ's and kicked back in the comfy Airstream couch surfing the internet. He even allowed himself a second cup of coffee today. It was during this second cup that he decided to look through old photos and delete the redundant ones that were just taking up space and memory. After all, he had Facebook as a backup for photos shared there and an automatic cloud account for all other photos on his phone. He just kept the ones that meant the most to him on his phone. Still, he had to go through the cloud account occasionally and weed those down too.

It occurred to him that if he had a backup on the cloud–and there were several options available, some coming free with your cell service and others being pay accounts–then maybe LaVoy had a backup account too. It was worth a shot.

He grabbed Takoda's card out of his junk drawer and called the number. He got the official recording: *This is Investigator Seth Armandarez of the Lakota Tribal Police. I am away from my desk at the moment. Please leave a message including your name, phone number and a case number and I will call you back as soon as I return...*

"Hey Takoda, hao kola, Mike Taylor here. I was just thinking, maybe our victim LaVoy has a photo cloud backup you can check. I use Google, but there are dozens of them: Dropbox, AT&T and the other cell companies give you so many gigs of cloud photo backup for free... Anyway, just a thought. Maybe I'll see you at the Pow Wow Saturday before I go to work... Peace out." he finished.

What Mike didn't yet know was that Takoda and his partner were busy. He didn't know about the scene at Janet Sweetwater's house, how her husband woke that morning and found her dead at the kitchen table, or how after the paramedics discovered ligature marks on her neck they called the Tribal Police, resulting in a four car response including Sergeant War Club and Senior Officer Tully Kangee Brown, or the response of Investigators Armandarez and Swallows. The whole neighborhood was out watching in this nice area of rez housing, most of the residents being tribal leaders and tribal government officials. Tully and the other officers interviewed several of the neighbors to no avail except for the next door neighbor who remembered a loud exhaust leaving that morning that he was not used to, a hefty V8 like a Mustang or a Charger...or a Camaro, Tully thought.

Mike had no idea there had been another murder that was most likely connected to the first. Rather, his thoughts after hanging up with Takoda were on watching Star dance on Saturday morning and having some fry bread. He was also chomping at the bit to ask War Club a whole slew of questions tomorrow at the Thunderbird Cafe, like about how Funmaker knew about him and where the hell his Airstream was parked. And what were Funmaker's connections to Phil Velardi?

Mike had half a mind to drive over to the Thunderbird for dinner on his night off just to hit War Club up about it… But a little later Frank walked over to the trailer while Mike was out with Max and invited him to come have some BBQ with him and the missus up on the patio, saying it would be getting too cold for that soon enough, and inquiring about the insulation in his fancy travel trailer for the winter. He decided to stay.

As Mike was getting himself properly dressed for dinner with the Trasks, Hobby and Tully were sitting down for their own dinner fare at the Thunderbird where they talked about the murders and Janet Sweetwater's connection to L & M Logistics, how this was obviously some attempt at a cover up, or just silencing a potential witness. They had no idea if she had her hands in the cookie jar or if she could just shed a lot of light on the contractor's orders on the rez. Their conversation turned to Mike Taylor and Hobby's manipulations, telling old Funmaker about the wasicu and his desire to sweat, his connection to Phil Velardi (who they knew by another name)...

"You gonna tell Taylor you're going to sweat with him next Wednesday?" Hobby asked.

"Nope," Tully answered before continuing, "You gonna tell him it was you put the bug in Funmaker's ear?"

"Nope," Hobby said.

Both men smiled as they finished their food.

As Mike went to bed that night around 10pm, his thoughts were on roll call tomorrow and his second full week at work. It was going pretty good so far... He knew he still had some work to do winning hearts and minds but he was somewhat confident in his leadership skills.

At about the same time Mike Taylor was turning in, Tully Kangee Brown was miles off the reservation in his Jeep, watching a small house through binoculars as two men got into a black Camaro and drove off towards the L & M Logistics warehouse for their evening shift. He waited for a while and then got out and walked around the block, going past the house on foot to see whatever there was to see. A flag pole with an American flag and a yellow *Don't Tread on Me* flag familiar to white supremacists and ex-military, a US Marine Corps sticker on both sides of the mailbox, and other small items including a heavy punching bag suspended in the carport next to the house with assorted free weights and a bench press told him pretty much what he wanted to know.

These men, at least the registered owner of the Camaro that came back to this address, were ex-military and they thought of themselves as patriots. Probably Marines and maybe Force Recon, definitely Infantry types that were proud of the Corps and stayed in shape. He didn't know who the second man was yet.

This was an unincorporated city and the house was older; the other cars were older too. Only the Camaro was shiny and new. So, these men had recently come up in life working for L & M or whomever... and they would be eager to prove themselves worthy. Tully wrote down the license plate numbers of the other cars parked on the property and out front on the street. There was someone else in the residence as he saw a TV flickering inside, but he didn't know who or how many there were. A girlfriend or wife maybe. He was in no hurry to get back to the rez, confirming they did in fact go to work. He'd get to that in time. The warehouse, one of them at least, was pretty much empty now. Box trucks and a few big rigs had been busy loading up whatever there was in there for a few days after the LaVoy murder, but they were done now. Only the other twin warehouse seemed to be doing business as usual. They had mostly electronic accessories in there, from keyboards and mouse pads to cables and chargers with another section of common school supplies like notebooks, paper, pens and pencils and even chalkboards.

Tully Kangee Brown had seen these types of shenanigans before from contractors on the rez. It wouldn't surprise him one bit if L & M Logistics suddenly closed down, lost their contracts and bids only to have another company jump right in and fill the void. In other words, all was status quo—making money off the Native American peoples. *Some things never change*, he thought.

Tully later drove by the warehouses and confirmed the Camaro was there. He then went to the station to run the plate numbers of the other vehicles before going home to bed. He would send Takoda and War Club an email of his findings.

"Hey Sarge, you got a second?" Deputy Johnson asked Mike as he sat outside the roll call room looking at the stack of reports he had to approve. They had been piling up in his in-box for the past three days.

Mike was early, which was his way. Johnson had come in early just to talk to him before their shift began. The deputy was already dressed, having just come out of the locker room, and was carrying a briefcase and a flashlight.

Mike motioned to the empty stool opposite where he was sitting at the long table.

"Have a seat. Welcome to my office!" he joked.

"Well," Johnson began timidly, "I was wondering about the sweat lodge thing… I know you told us you grew up going to sweat lodge, and was wondering if you are going to be going to a lodge out here somewhere."

"I am actually. Something kind of popped up out of the blue. What is your first name by the way? This isn't the military. We can use first names," Mike said.

"Jason, but Johnson is fine," he answered.

"What's your Lakota name?"

"My mother's last name was Red Tail Feather. She called me Chatan when I was young, but I've never really gone by that. I was not born on the reservation. My dad is an investment banker, met my mom her first year at university. They got married and that was that." he said.

"Chatan, that means hawk. That's a good name! Are you a member of the tribe?"

"Ah, no. Like I said, I've never lived on the reservation. But lately I've been thinking a lot about my Indian side, but to get enrolled in the tribe it's kind of complicated: you have to present evidence, birth certificates and all that. You have to be at least fifty percent."

"First off, you can enroll if you want to. I think with the DNA companies like 23 and Me and Ancestry and all, proving fifty percent should be easy enough. If your dad has just a few percent you're over that hump. Secondly, *Indian* is considered a derogatory term these days. You are Native American or of the First Nations. Be proud of that. I can certainly ask to bring you to Inipi. I just helped Leksi (Lek-she), *Uncle*, build a new Inipi and spruce up his old grounds on the rez and I will be going to my first sweat in a few months this Wednesday. I'll float the idea with him. I know he has invited a few folks to sweat, don't know how many, but I'm sure he will agree. Just let me feel things out first, okay?"

"Yeah sure. Is it true you've been working with the Tribal Police on a murder investigation? Rumor has it you've been out there on the rez the last three days on your RDO's working side by side with the TP. We've like never done that! I think it's pretty cool but a few of the fellas in roll call said you're going to get your ass shot out there," Johnson smiled wide.

"Ah, that is not true actually. I'll have to address that in roll call. I'll leave your name out of it. Oh, people are arriving to work, let's talk hockey. How 'bout them Kings?" Mike asked.

"Who?" Johnson responded.

Roll call went well. Mike did address the rumors, explaining that he was in contact with the TP on the case of the Native American man dumped over the fence last week but no, he had not been on the rez to help in the investigation. He had been on the rez to build a sweat lodge with a Native American spiritual leader and planned to attend sweat lodge next week, but that was the extent of his forays onto the reservation. He did tell them that there was a Pow Wow this weekend and all were invited, that if they had never had fry bread tacos they were really missing out. He told everyone to go to work and to be safe. He then went back out to the table and sat down to go through paperwork. He no longer had his Airstream close by to use as his impromptu substation. He signed off on everything, noting the reports were looking a little better, and found an envelope with something inside addressed to him. Inside he found a small US Army lapel pin. He smiled and put it on his shirt. He knew it was Deputy Yancy Rivera that had sent it to him. He'd thank her tomorrow. She was off today.

Mike finally got in the field an hour later. The radio was quiet other than a few report calls as soon as the shift got into the field: a theft report and a hit-and-run of a parked vehicle. He drove around for a while and headed over to the

Thunderbird Cafe at the appointed time to hit up War Club. He was fairly sure it was the cagey old sergeant that had set things in motion...

The hostess was all smiles as he came in. She sure had a pretty face, and that hair! She pointed back to where Hobby was sitting by himself in the highly coveted rear booth.

"Hey, sergeant wasicu! Have a seat, lots to talk about!" he teased.

"Yeah, I've got a bone to pick with you too Injun Joe, like who sent Funmaker to my trailer to start with?"

The white couple in the booth next to them turned to look at the two feuding policemen from different agencies. They weren't sure if they were kidding or not.

"It's okay," Mike said to the worried looking civilians, "he's my brother from another mother."

"Ha! Why, I don't know what you're talking about! Funmaker? Never heard of him! How's that old truck of his running?" Hobby asked.

"I knew it!" Mike said.

"At any rate, that will have to wait a minute. We've had another murder and this time it was someone much more important on the rez. People are now watching, calling for the FBI to take over!"

"What?" Mike settled down and looked at Hobby intently.

Hobby then laid things out to Mike, speaking a bit more softly, telling him about Janet Sweetgrass and her murder.

Then he told Mike about the Camaro and its occupants, everything Tully had emailed him and Takoda. They ordered and their food arrived, all while Hobby was telling him everything that had transpired. Finally, Hobby told him Takoda got his message and was looking into that photo app. That was a darn good idea, he added.

"So, is Takoda going to hook those guys up, get a warrant, or what? I know he didn't share that Camaro bit with Barton, by the way. He's going to have to eventually..."

"I can neither confirm nor deny these baseless accusations, whiteman. You going to Pow Wow tomorrow? I probably won't make it here next two days. I'll be at the Pow Wow on duty. You can ask Takoda there. He'll be there. He goes to lodge too, you know. He runs one! Very spiritual guy!"

"I didn't know that. That's good to know. What about you? Do you sweat?" he asked the older man.

"Yeah, when I take out the trash. My wife is Catholic–you know, Jesus, the white medicine man. She drags me to church every month or so."

Pow Wow

Takoda sat at his desk rereading the email he'd just written to Detective Barton, his finger hovering over the send button. He'd shared everything to date with the detective, including the new murder and its possible connection to the case Barton was working jointly with the Tribal Police, and for the first time, he'd added the bit about the black Camaro. He laid it all out, the video footage, *not giving a date on exactly when that was discovered,* and subsequent investigation into the plate and registered owner of the vehicle, including the surveillance of said residence and findings there, to include the possible second suspect. Takoda suggested Barton move quickly to obtain both warrants for their arrests and for the search of the residence for any and all related items.

He had little doubt that Barton was going to flip his lid about not being notified immediately, and he was also fairly sure Barton would drag his feet, but this was off the reservation and he needed him to get the warrants. He just hoped the County Sheriff's Detective wouldn't spoil the investigation or go over there without warrants and spook the two suspected murderers into skipping town. He left the part about the photos he'd just discovered on the victim's cloud backup service out of the email. He had to verify that first, afterall, but it was Saturday and he only stopped by his office at Tribal Police Headquarters to compose and send the email before heading over to the Pow Wow.

Reluctantly, he pushed send.

Mike stuffed his uniform and duty belt in his gym bag, told Max he was in charge of the Airstream, and headed off to the Pow Wow before work. He arrived a little after ten o'clock and was happy to see people still arriving, booths still being set up. He decided the first order of business was going to be fry bread tacos. He saw other white people so he was happy he wouldn't be getting dirty looks. Or, so he thought. He realized it was the shirt he was wearing. People would look at the shirt, then at his white wasicu face as he headed over and got in line at one of the food booths. They weren't all bad looks. Some people smiled and a few had no reaction at all.

At the head of the line, some three people in front of him, he saw a tall Native American that looked familiar; with his back turned, however, Mike couldn't quite place him. He recognized the girl's voice waiting on him by her cheerfulness, and as she stepped away to grab the man's order he saw that it was the hostess from the Thunderbird

Cafe. Great, he thought...this wasn't going to be awkward at all. Then the man turned his head and he realized it was Tully.

"Boy, they'll let anyone get tacos here won't they? Even Tribal Police!" Mike said jokingly.

Tully turned around farther to see who had made the off handed comment, that stoic look on his face and smiled himself at seeing Mike a few people back.

"Hey hey, you made it! Washte, *good*. Meet me over at the tables." Tully said, as he turned back to get his order.

Mike made it up to the front of the line in a few minutes to see his favorite hostess face to face.

"Hi Mike! It's nice to see you here. No work today?" she asked, smiling bright.

"Later. I wanted to stop by and have some fry bread tacos and watch some dancing first."

"That's great!" she said, looking at his shirt, but continuing to smile.

He collected his food and then walked over to the community benches nearby. Hobby was in uniform standing next to where Tully was sitting. He was finishing his last taco.

"Oh, you are *not* wearing a Free Leonard Peltier shirt!" Hobby said, at seeing the controversial T-shirt.

Leonard Peltier was a Native American political prisoner and member of the American Indian Movement, convicted in the slayings of two FBI agents on an Indian

Reservation in 1975. His other co-conspirators were actually found not guilty in a trial that followed the shootings. However, Leonard was on the run and hiding out, up in Canada. When he was finally caught and extradited back to the United States, the FBI and Prosecuting Attorneys had plenty of time to lick their wounds and learn from their mistakes from the first trial. In a highly contested and controversial trial, Leonard Peltier was convicted of the killings. The FBI's lead witness, however, wanted to recant her testimony in the case, claiming she was threatened and had a low IQ; there were also problems with the FBI's forensic evidence. A documentary called *Incident at Oglala*, made by none other than famed actor and director Robert Redford, documented well the problems with the government's case against Leonard.

"Yeah, what's wrong with it?" Mike asked.

"I don't know if anyone told you, but you're *white*," Hobby whispered, jokingly.

"I guess I can turn it inside out? I don't have another T shirt with me...wait, I have my white T in the Tahoe with my uniform. I'll go change," he said.

"Do you really think he should be freed?" Tully asked him.

"Ah, yes, yes I do. I mean I think he was there, he may have even fired the coup de gras, but that trial was bullshit. I may be a cop, but I recognize a bad trial when I see it. The law isn't supposed to work that way," he finished.

"Then wear it! Sit down and eat your tacos, they're getting cold," Tully said.

Mike sat down and started to eat.

Hobby just stood there smiling, "I saw you talking to Chapawee Lucinda, your favorite hostess, I think you should ask her out. She likes you."

"That's her name! Lucinda. What does Chapawee mean again? It sounds familiar but..."

"Basically, it means *does a lot*, or *industrious*. It's her nickname because she is so smart," Hobby said.

"She is pretty. That hair! But I just got here and she looks so young!" Mike balked, not even mentioning that he thought the girl was a bit on the curvy side. Native American men don't have the same thoughts on the matter he knew. Skinny blondes with blue eyes and a valley girl accent were pretty much SoCal white, Mike thought, realizing he too held preconceived prejudices that he wasn't previously aware of. He knew he had more spiritual work to do.

"She's 22," Tully spoke up, "she just finished her Master's in child psychology and is about to start her doctorate program. She's just helping out her parents at the Thunderbird—she took a semester off. But don't ask her out. Whites should stay with whites," he finished, looking up at Hobby with that stoic look of his for suggesting the match.

"What?" Hobby said in defense, throwing his hands up in the air.

Hobby said he needed to go do some rounds and walked off, shaking his head. Mike sat and ate in silence, drinking his coke. It had just become awkward between him and the big Indian.

"I'm not racist. I'm a member of a dwindling nation. Jews stick together to preserve their ways. I just believe my people need to marry within as well... Maybe I'm a little racist, but I'm sitting with you aren't I? And I'm going to sweat with you next week too," he said.

Mike looked up at the bigger man in surprise.

"Oh," was all he could manage.

Tully said he had some friends to check on but that Mike should head down to the ring when he hears the drums if he wanted to see the girl's dancing.

Mike finished his fry bread tacos and threw away his trash. He knew they weren't really traditional Lakota food, but they sure were good. He started walking around to the various booths to check out the fair. There were a lot of nice shirts and handmade gifts, jewelry, and other items for sale. He continued to get looks on his shirt but he ignored it. At eleven o'clock on the nose, he heard a drum beat start up at the dancing circle off to one side of the Pow Wow grounds. He walked that way.

Mike didn't know the first thing about Lakota dancing or how it was judged but he guessed he was about to find out. Almost twenty years of going to sweat lodge had taught him a lot about Lakota spirituality but that was it. He realized that in moving here he had a lot to learn about the Lakota people and their daily lives.

As he made his way to the circle he decided to turn to the left and go around towards the side where there were some low rise bleachers set up that only stood about six feet high and allowed four rows of seating. He saw three youngsters in their late teens or early twenties standing next to the dancing area checking out people as they walked by. They looked like troublemakers Mike noted, up to no good.

When he approached them the lead Lakota youth spotted Mike's shirt and nudged one of his friends.

"Oh, we got one of *those!* Hey wasicu, what tribe are you? You from the *Wannabe* tribe?"

His two friends laughed at the joke, suggesting that Mike was one of those white people that act like they are native but are not; members of the *Wanna-be an Indian* nation. Mike just smiled and did not respond. But, as he passed them he noticed that the one that had spoken wasn't kidding. He genuinely looked angry.

It was bound to happen, he knew. Someone was going to attack him verbally. Not like Star had scolded him about trying to teach her son Lakota legends at the Thunderbird either. This was some real hostility.

"Yeah keep walking, *Dances with Wolves!*" the young man said as he continued on, looking for a seat.

He spotted Tully sitting in the far right top corner of the risers next to another man in civilian clothes. The man's head was turned towards Tully, telling him something. As he got closer he recognized the man was Takoda, who made eye contact with him and smiled, waiving him up to sit with them. He wasn't too sure Tully wanted to sit with him–maybe he was being over sensitive, but Takoda wanted him to come over so he did. *Cops were cops*, he thought as he climbed up the risers. They always want to be in the back, no one behind them. It didn't matter what race they were either.

"Nice shirt!" Takoda said, smiling as usual, so Mike wasn't sure if he meant it or not, but he was leaning towards the former, "What did Angry Boy say to you down there?"

"Angry Boy, you can say that again!" Mike said as he sat down, "He didn't like my shirt, called me a wannabe Indian. I'm used to that. No big deal."

"Used to that? Who else has been giving you a hard time since you moved here? I think it's refreshing to meet a white man that's on the Red Road and is humble about it. The wannabes try to be Indian, claim their great-grandmother was a Cherokee princess and so on. You don't do that. Don't worry about those three–they are just bored," Takoda said.

Mike was touched by Takoda's words.

"I don't know the first thing about being Lakota. I just know how to beat the drum, sing a few songs in the setting of the inipi is all. Like this dancing and singing competition today, I don't know how it's judged or anything. I've sweated with Native Americans that didn't want to sweat with me because I was white. Sometimes I just tended the fire that day or they reluctantly decided to go in with me. Uncle always told me to ignore that stuff, don't let it take me off my journey."

"Good advice. I'd like to meet your *uncle:* he sounds knowledgeable. As to the dancing today, the women will start first. They are competitive and trying to get to the big national competition where there is some serious prize money! This is the last qual. Now, there are three kinds of dancers. You have the Traditional dancers: see some of the ladies have a shawl over one arm and are holding a feather fan in the other?" he pointed towards the female dancers that were filling the sides of the ring, spreading out as they came in, "Then you have the Fancy Shawl dancers there and finally you have the Jingle Dress dancers which is self-explanatory. They are my favorite. It was a medicine man that invented that dance. It came to him in a vision to cure a sick young girl, so he had the dresses made and they danced and low and behold the girl was cured. A hundred years later the Jingle Dress is still around! Now, as to judging...yeah, no one really knows for sure. Tully, what do you think?" he asked, turning towards the big man.

Tully shrugged his shoulders, "I have no idea. I think it changes with the judges but you know, we know who did the best dance."

Just then an announcement was made over some crude speakers that they would be starting in a few minutes, giving the older folks time to get to the grounds and find a seat, asking for patience.

"Hey, what about those photos? Did you find anything?" Mike asked Takoda.

"Ah, glad you asked. You're a genius by the way," Takoda said as he fished his phone out of his top pocket, "Mrs. LaVoy said he did have backup service and she even had his password–it was their anniversary date sadly enough… Here, look at this!"

Mike took the phone as Takoda passed it to him and looked at the screen. It showed two long rows of washers and dryers, dozens of them, and against the far wall there were thousands of laptop computers stacked on big industrial shelving units.

"Washers and computers? I don't understand."

"Theft, Mike. It's as simple as that. Think about it. We don't need that many units. Imagine how many Speed King washers and dryers must have been in that warehouse! Hundreds? Those are top-of-the-line washers and dryers! And how many computers are in there? Someone is working the system. Jannet Sweetwater knows how many units were ordered, or supposed to be ordered and now she's dead. It's the oldest trick in the book: making money off of the Indian people. Someone is changing the numbers and selling off the overage for big money. They've been doing this shit since they put us on reservations! Indian Agents ordering a ton of food and beef, giving us the rotted scraps! I just hope Barton does his job! I sent over everything this morning. We need those guys arrested, leaned on for info, their house searched!"

"So, you told him about the Camaro then?" Mike said. Takoda smiled.

"Yeah, I told him. You caught that, did you? You're alright with me, Red Road," Takoda said.

"He's okay," Tully added.

"Who are the two guys? Who killed LaVoy and the woman?" Mike asked.

"They are brothers, Troy and David Loller. David is an ex-felon, Troy was a Marine–Force Recon in Afghanistan. My money is on him for both killings; his Facebook page is full of American Patriot, borderline White Supremacist bullshit. I made his brother from his photos and posts. Couldn't find a Facebook or any other social media for David, just his record for B & E (Breaking & Entering). But if Barton doesn't get those warrants today I think L & M is going to fold up and go away. They'll bring in another company and just resume business."

"Wow! You've been busy! Who got the plate on the Camaro? And did you scope out the residence?" Mike asked.

Takoda motioned with his left thumb over at Tully, "Our former Army Scout here. He loves that stuff."

"Outstanding!" Mike said.

The Jingle Dancers made their way out onto the dirt ring, their dresses jingling, each dancer wearing a number so the judges could identify them. Mike noticed Star was right in the front row, almost dead center. A drum beat started, followed by men singing in Lakota, and the ladies began to dance. All talk of the case stopped as Mike watched in amazement. Star was fantastic. Her body moved with the drum beat, her dress jingling from hundreds of handmade metal cone shaped bells sewn onto it as she danced, her feet gliding over the ground, barely kicking up any dust as if she was floating. Twice, she made eye contact with him as she smiled and danced, looking out over the spectators.

Halfway through the dance Mike looked over and saw Angry Boy looking up at him, mad-dogging him. He looked over at Takoda and pointed towards the troubled young man. Takoda nodded and continued watching the dance till it ended. The audience clapped and cheered, some whistled and others called out the names of the dancers and their relation to them.

"Excuse me," Takoda said as he got up and made his way down the risers and walked over to Angry Boy and his cohort.

The Jingle dancers moved off the floor and the Traditional dancers moved onto it.

"What's that all about?" Tully asked.

"Angry boy was glaring at me while Star was dancing."

"Oh, you know one of the girls. That explains it. Wichahpi-Star White Cloud is his sister. Raymond Angry Boy is a bit of a hot-head. Takoda will sort him out."

Mike watched as Takoda approached the three. They looked a bit sheepish suddenly as Takoda began speaking quietly to them. It was odd, Mike thought. No bravado now, as if he was a tribal elder or something. The two cohorts looked down at their feet and Angry Boy pointed up at Mike but didn't seem to raise his voice or argue while talking to Takoda. The drumbeat started for the Traditional dancers and Takoda turned and walked back up the risers. The three troublemakers walked out of the dance area.

Takoda was smiling as he came back up the risers, "Did he really call you, *Dances with Wolves?"*

"Yeah," Mike answered.

"That's funny," Takoda said as he nudged past Mike's legs and retook his seat.

"Is that why you started sweating, after watching that movie?" Tully asked.

"No. In all fairness that's a darn good movie! Kevin Costner and Graham Greene did a great job in that! But I started sweating at 10. I didn't see that movie until I was like 20 years old."

"Good movie," Takoda echoed, "But what about the PostMan? That wasn't so good."

"I don't know, I liked it, but I'm pretty easily entertained. I like most of Kevin Costner's movies," Mike said.

"Water World?" Takota asked.

"Oh, that sucked!" Tully chimed in.

"Okay, Water World was not so good," Mike answered.

"Open Range," Tully mentioned, "That was his best movie."

"Yeah," both Mike and Takoda agreed.

The drums began and they sat back and watched more dancing. All in all, they sat there for almost two hours, talking during breaks, though not so much about the case now as the risers filled up with people. Mike looked at the time on his phone and said he had to take off soon for work. The young girls were dancing now and they were very cute but he had to go. He got up to leave and waved to Tully. Takoda got up too and followed him down and out of the arena area into the maze of booths and food trailers. They saw the three trouble-makers who definitely saw them too but they looked down or away, as if they didn't want any problem with Takoda.

"Why are those guys so afraid of you? Because you're Five-O." referring to his status as a Tribal Police Investigator.

Takoda laughed at the Hawaii Five-O reference, "No, it's because I'm a spiritual leader and Angry Boy and the other two sometimes sweat with me. I'm trying to pull them away from being angry Indians. We have enough of those, members of the *movement* and all that militant crap!"

"Oh, I didn't know that. What did you tell them, may I ask?"

"Well, I asked them why they were giving my white friend a hard time and Angry Boy said that you, he called you *Dances with Wolves,* were staring at his sister while she was dancing. I said we were all staring at Star because she's a great dancer and she's pretty, duh!"

"Well, thanks, you didn't have to do that," Mike said.

"You're either on the Red Road and being humble, grateful, and kind, or you're on the Black Road. You can't be on both. I told him that too and told him to go sweat with you this Wednesday at Funmaker's trailer, get his mind right or he can't come back to my lodge."

Mike didn't know what to say to that.

They saw Hobby War Club standing over by the food tables with another uniformed Tribal Policeman that Mike had not yet met and started that way. Mike wanted to say goodbye, even though he planned to come back tomorrow to watch some male dancing and drumming. He loved listening to Lakota songs on the drum like the Flag song and the Friendship song; they had been familiar to him his whole life it seemed. You could feel the drumbeat in your chest. He knew a great little child's lullaby played on a hand drum called the star child song. He hoped to maybe teach it to Benny, Star's son, if he ever worked up the courage to ask her out...

Hobby introduced the other officer and they all talked a bit. Mike said he had to get going, but then he saw Star walking towards them. They all turned towards her as she approached the group of men.

"Can I talk to you for a minute?" she asked Mike.

"Sure, anytime," he said and walked towards her as she turned and walked a few feet away from the group before turning around. She was still wearing the beautiful Jingle Dress and the bells jingled away as she walked, especially when she turned.

"Did my brother give you a hard time? I saw him glaring at you while I was dancing. I saw Takoda go down and talk to him too. I want to apologize–he's a bit of a hothead. I guess I am too. I want to apologize for snapping at you at the Thunderbird the other day. We're a traditional family. I don't hate whites, just what whites have done to us in the past–like Wounded Knee, you know? He doesn't know you're the sheriff that speaks Lakota. I just told him that you're a good guy."

Mike was happy she had sought him out to apologize. He was wondering if this was a good time to ask her out or if he should let that sit for a while. He turned his head to see three Lakota men, his friends, just a few feet back staring at them, probably listening to every word they said so he decided this was not the time.

"I understand. No hard feelings. Hey, where is Benny? Why isn't he watching his mom dance? You were amazing by the way. This is my first time watching Lakota dance. Your Jingle Dress is beautiful."

"Oh, thanks!" she blushed slightly, "He's at home with my mom. Trust me, he sees me dancing in the front room all the time! Well, I gotta get back for the judging. I'll see you around?"

"Sure, sure. See you at the Thunderbird probably?" he said, lamely. He didn't know what to say or how to end it.

"Bye then," she waved and turned with a jingle and walked away.

Mike walked back to the group of men eyeing him suspiciously now.

"Ooh la la! What's that all about, Sheriff Taylor? Aunt Bea know about this?" Hobby teased.

"Nothing. She just wanted to apologize for her brother and for snapping at me last week at the cafe," he said.

"I didn't hear about that." Takoda said, looking at Hobby.

"Tell ya later," Hobby told him.

Mike said goodbye, saying he wanted to get a few more tacos for the road. He then walked over to the booth selling fry bread tacos and ordered 3 more tacos and another coke.

"I saw Star talking to you just now. What was that?" Lucinda asked him with a smile.

"Oh her brother made some remarks at my whiteness… She apologized for him and for snapping at me at the Thunderbird last week. I sort of deserved it, telling Benny what the eagle feather stands for…"

"Oh, okay. She's a friend of mine. Do you want me to talk to her for you?"

"No, it's fine. What about you? How many tacos have

you had today working here? I wouldn't be able to control myself!" He regretted saying that as soon as it came out of his mouth.

"Not one! I'm on a diet! I gained twenty pounds being home this semester. Time to lose a few pounds before I go back to school!"

"What are you talking about? You are a beautiful girl!" he said, trying to make her feel better.

A couple with two kids came up behind him and he got out of the way. He told Lucinda he'd see her Monday at the Thunderbird.

He turned and walked towards the parking lot, Hobby making eye contact with him, still standing by the tables with the other officer. He pointed his fingers at his eyes and then at Mike, symbolizing he was watching him.

Wants & Warrants and the FBI

Sunday at the Pow Wow was, thankfully, less confrontational. For one thing, Mike wore a less controversial shirt. For another, there was no sign of Raymond Angry Boy and his friends. There was also no sign of Star, unfortunately. Tully and Hobby were there, both on duty, and Lucinda was her usual chipper self in the food booth, so it turned out to be a good morning. They watched the men's dance and listened to some drum songs so loud that people out in the parking lot could hear them perfectly clear.

As he strolled through the grounds Mike was very happy to see that Star had won the Jingle Dress competition and would be moving on to represent the tribe in future competitions. Her name was posted with the other winners and alternates on a bulletin board down by the dance ring.

Mike ate more fry bread tacos and talked to the boys, ribbing them about this and that. He called Hobby an overtime whore, working this easy assignment on his day off after Hobby had told him he was going to get fat on all that fry bread. It was all good kidding around, although Mike refrained from teasing Tully about anything. Tully was a spiritual man like himself and more reserved than he was, plus, he really didn't know where he stood with the big man. Hobby was easy: he was a kidder and obviously a meddler, but in a good way. Mike was thinking of giving Hobby a new Lakota nickname, something like, "gets in others business," or something like that, when Lucinda came over on a break and asked Mike how everything was.

Tully and Hobby took that as a sign and left to walk around the grounds in their official capacity as Tribal Policemen.

She sat down opposite Mike and they made small talk. She asked him how he liked the little intertribal Pow Wow and how he was finding his new job and the South Dakota area. He asked her when she started school again and how far of a drive it was. She said not to worry, that she would be home on weekends and it wasn't far to university, that she could drive home daily if she wanted to. But she enjoyed dorm living because she didn't lose time on the road and that there were plenty of friends to study with, and being a graduate student, she got a lot more perks like a room to herself, no curfew and access to more areas of the university.

She really was nice. She was pretty too and didn't seem to care one bit that he was wasicu.

As he left for work and roll call he was now feeling conflicted.

Star or Lucinda, Lucinda or Star?

After roll call Mike walked out to the sergeant's SUV to go in service. As he unlocked and opened the door the siren went off. It made him jump. He hurriedly climbed in and yanked the fishing line off the activation arm and turned it off. He smiled, heart racing. How many times had he done this same rat pack on other officers back in Santa Ana? he wondered with a grin on his face. It was one of the oldest tricks in the book: enter the car from the passenger side, loop the fishing line around the activation bar and something smooth on the passenger side like the shotgun barrel, then loop it back to the driver's door. When the driver opens the door–voila! He is greeted by an ear piercing siren.

Probably the twins, he surmised. *Well, at least one of them…*

Whoever it was, they would tip their hand, say something to betray their actions. Hell, they were probably watching or, worse yet, had filmed it on their cell phone.

Mike looked around the unit parking area behind the department but didn't see anyone.

He drove around for a while, checking out new areas while thinking of how he was going to get even. Oh, he would get even, he thought. There was one particular rat pack from his Santa Ana days that stuck out in his mind involving a stuffed alligator. That alligator was used over and over to get people. He needed to come up with something equally spectacular.

Deputy Ahern asked for a Spanish speaker and Mike picked up his mic and said he was en route. Ahern had called in a car stop a few minutes before. *Very good*, he thought as he rolled that way. His deputies were calling in their stops. Translation was fairly uncomplicated. Ahern had written the driver a citation and the driver claimed to not speak any English, a common tactic back in California by people of other nationalities thinking if they claim no knowledge of the language they could either get out of a ticket or not show up to court and later claim they just didn't understand the process to the judge. Mike told the man what the citation was for and the court date, showing him this on the bottom of the ticket and had him sign it.

When Mike told dispatch he was back in service they advised him that Detective Barton wanted to make contact with him in the Watch Commander's Office. Wow, Mike thought, Barton was working on a Sunday. He took that as a good sign. He returned to the station and walked to the office where the relief Lieutenant, whom he didn't know very well, was sitting with Barton.

"Sergeant Taylor!" Barton began upon seeing him, "What are you doing at 0700 tomorrow morning?"

"Sleeping?" Mike ventured.

"Nope. Call your sneaky pal Armandarez and have him and his partner meet us here at 7am. We're serving the warrant on the house with four detectives and half of dayshift, you and the two detectives from TP. I just got everything signed by the duty judge. It's easier on weekends actually. We're already behind the 8 ball on this one, should have done it Friday but your pal wasn't forthcoming on that Camaro business. Those two should be home at that time."

"Ah...okay, I'll call him now. Why not hit them now? They don't go in, if they are going in at all, till just before 10pm?"

"Why would you say, 'if they are going in at all'? What am I missing? What else aren't you guys telling me?"

"Oh. Just that L & M has emptied out that warehouse and only the other warehouse filled with school supplies seems to be operating now…"

"God damn it! And your Indian pals accused us of not sharing! Well it's too late. I already set everything in motion for 0700! So, we'll see what we get then."

Barton got up in a huff and started to walk out.

"Is it okay if I put out a BOLO on the Camaro? Patrol may be able to scoop them up tonight."

"Do what you want!" he barked as he walked down the hall, "Call me at home if you get them!"

The relief Lieutenant sat back with his arms folded, looking at Mike.

"And that's why we don't work with the tribals. I don't care for those Indians over there too much but the brass upstairs is all aflutter over hiring you and your quick connection with the Indian Nation. So good luck with that *Sergeant.*"

"Yes sir," Mike said, not knowing what to say to the relief Lieutenant's negativity.

Mike excused himself and walked over to dispatch and gave the information to them to put out over the radio. He also asked the two dispatchers if they needed anything, but they declined. His years of experience had taught him it was better to be on their good side. He walked back to his unit and got out of the area of the department as quickly as he could.

A few minutes later, dispatch put out the BOLO information:

"Attention all units, prepare to copy the following: Be on the Lookout for a Black Chevrolet Camaro, SD license plate #KMA-148, wanted in connection with a 22-16-4 *murder* investigation. Occupants should be considered armed and dangerous."

Mike drove over to the VFW post and parked in the back parking lot. It was familiar territory. He pulled out his cell phone and called Takoda, got the familiar message, and left word with him at the beep. He wasn't sure Takoda would get the message in time so he called Hobby.

"Sergeant War Club. Whom do I have the pleasure of speaking to?"

"Hobby, Mike Taylor here. Hey, I need a big favor!"

"No Sergeant Taylor, I'm not bringing you any more tacos! You have had enough!" he chided. Mike could hear someone chuckle in the background.

"No, seriously, the warrants on the Loller brothers are active and I need to get a hold of Takoda. Barton is hitting the house tomorrow morning and Takoda and Swallows are invited. They need to be at the department at 0700. I left a message for him but I don't know if he will get it in time."

"Oh! That was fast. I didn't think ole Barton had it in him. At any rate, I'll call him on his personal cell and let him know," Hobby said.

"We put out a BOLO on the radio for the Camaro too, just now, so if you guys see it on the rez, light them up! Armed and dangerous of course."

"Yea, yea, what's the plate on that? I don't have the info with me. I mean other than two white creeps in a black Camaro!"

"KMA-148. What are you doing right now?" Mike asked, trying to be more familiar.

"We're still at the Pow Wow grounds. They're wrapping things up, taking things down. I'm going to release Tully and Walker now. I'll have them go check the warehouse. I'll save your number in my phone thingy here."

Mike told Hobby to be safe and hung up. He sat in his

car for a few minutes trying to calm down. Things were moving fast now. He knew most of his deputies, the good ones, had already run that plate and were in the process of checking out the residence of the registered owner for that car. He would drive by there himself a few times during the rest of the night, but first he wanted to go in and sit for a while, get a cup of coffee at the bar.

1800 hours, *6pm,* Mike received a text from an unsaved number on his phone.

"Message received. Meet you at department 0700. Takoda."

Mike texted back an acknowledgement and saved the number to his phone. He was glad Takoda now trusted him enough to share his private number with him.

1943 hours, *7:43pm,* Deputy Frank Martinez spotted the Camaro getting off the highway onto a surface street, headed towards the residence.

"Pine 312! I have the wanted Camaro, just got off route 6! I'm southbound on Gilbert!" he shouted excitedly over the radio.

Mike knew this wasn't Santa Ana where felony car stops were a dime a dozen, happening all day, everyday, and officers were generally used to that and sounded much calmer over the radio. Hell, this could be Martinez's first felony car stop ever. He had no way of knowing…

"Emergency radio traffic only," dispatch began, "Any unit in the area to follow, Pine 312 is following a wanted vehicle southbound Gilbert from route 6."

"Don't light him up yet," Mike said to himself as he punched it and started that way. He was four miles out.

"…ine 311 en route. I'm two blocks away!" Deputy Rivera responded, the beginning of her transmission cut off by not waiting the required half a second to talk after keying her mic.

"Pine 301 en route from a distance," Mike said, "Don't light him up till you get another unit behind you."

"Failure to yield!" Martinez shouted over the radio, "In pursuit! He's whipping a U turn, I think we're headed back to the interstate!"

"Damn it!" Mike said to himself as he pushed the Ford Explorer as fast as he dared on the rural streets.

Martinez wasn't experienced enough to know to wait for another officer or two before engaging a wanted vehicle.

"Copy, vehicle now Northbound Gilbert towards route 6," dispatch echoed.

Deputy Rivera headed straight for the onramp to route 6, arriving just as Martinez took the ramp, fishtailing his big Ford Crown Victoria behind the more nimble Camaro. The two vehicles were a hundred yards ahead of her, merging onto the highway as she took the ramp. She saw what looked like a puff of smoke come from the passenger side of the Camaro, a silvery metallic object hanging out the window briefly.

"Shots fired!" Martinez shouted, "My windshield is shattered! I can't see!"

"Copy, shots fired. All units, shots fired," dispatch announced.

"Martinez, pull over and stop," Mike said in the clear, not taking time in the midst of an emergency to use proper radio call signs.

"Pine 311, I'm now lead vehicle," Rivera said, much calmer than Martinez, her siren wailing in the background along with engine noise.

"301, do we have an air unit available?" Mike asked dispatch.

"Negative. We'll check with State Patrol."

Deputy Rivera stayed way to the left side of the Camaro as she attempted to overtake it. She wanted to stay out of the passenger's direct line of fire back towards her vehicle. Smart thinking, tactically, but it was of no use. Her Crown Vic was no match for the horsepower of the sleek Camaro.

"Pine 311, I've lost sight of the vehicle," she said, obvious disappointment in her voice.

"301, anything on that airship?" Mike asked.

"301, be advised, fixed wing aircraft en route, ETA five minutes," dispatch said.

"301 copy that, give them the info on the vehicle and last known location, direction of travel, break, 311 terminate your pursuit," Mike said. He threw the microphone at the dash in frustration. It bounced off and landed on the passenger floorboard.

"Damn!" he said.

"Pine 311 copy, terminating pursuit," Rivera said, her usual professionalism returning.

Mike stopped by and checked on Martinez on the side of route 6. Other than a light dusting of glass particles from the windshield breaking, he was fine, if a little excited still. He'd probably never been shot at in his life. He said he was fine and called for a tow truck. Mike sat in his vehicle waiting for the tow so he could give Martinez a lift with his equipment back to the department. He would need another vehicle to finish his shift. He texted Hobby and Takoda– then called dispatch and asked them to call Detective Barton at home and advise him of the pursuit of the suspects and have him advise on the search warrant. Mike was sure he would want to move the search time up but dispatch called him back five minutes later and said the 0700 time was still a go. *Lazy*, Mike thought, *Just lazy*.

At 0700 hours the next morning, Mike met Takoda and Swallows in the lobby and took them to the briefing room where several dedicated patrol deputies were gathered waiting for Barton and the other detectives. They were... fashionably late.

Barton and three other detectives walked in at 17 minutes past the hour and began the briefing, asking Mike to tell everyone what had happened last night. Mike stood up and introduced himself and then took it a step further and introduced Investigators' Armandarez and Swallows from the Lakota Tribal Police. He then told everyone what had transpired the night before, adding that State Patrol were UTL (unable to locate) on the suspect vehicle and that the search this morning was probably a formality as they would have surely called the residence by now and sanitized it. He made eye contact with Barton twice while saying that last part.

For the dayshift deputies, this was their first look at Mike Taylor, the lateral from California that spoke Lakota. Mike got a lot of looks as did Takoda and Swallows. A TP officer or investigator may have stopped by from time to time to pull records or talk to the watch commander or shift sergeant, but sitting in on a briefing and participating in a search warrant? This was all new to them. Feelings were decidedly mixed towards Sergeant Mike Taylor: some of the deputies liked the forward progress, but most resented it out of typical neophobic response. Cops really don't like change, even if it's good.

Barton handed out assignments for the search, and at

0750 hours Detective Barton and his partner led the cara-
van of vehicles out of the back parking lot and proceeded to
the residence. Vehicles took up half the street as the deputies and officers descended on the home giving knock and
notice. Barton actually waited for the woman in the house
to answer the door rather than use the *door key,* a handheld
battering ram, perhaps knowing he had messed up by not
hitting the residence last night right after the pursuit. Or,
more likely, Detective Barton was merely lazy.

The woman acted shocked but appeared ready for it.
She had been well coached as she protested and came outside already dressed in a coat and holding a small child. She
was ushered off to the side of the front yard and the deputies and officers went inside to start the search, a few remaining outside for security, one standing with the woman.
Mike was assigned to ensure all personnel were doing their
jobs: searching in the right places, reporting all finds to the
log officer, and tagging and bagging everything properly.

After 30 minutes or so, not much had been found other
than a few laptops and a few boxes of military grade 5.56
ammunition they dug out of a toolbox in the carport area.
Nothing obvious or directly related to the killings of LaVoy
or Sweetwater were found and it would take weeks to go
through the computers.

Just before 0900 hours, two men in dark suits wearing
aviator sunglasses walked up the driveway where a deputy
stopped them. They identified themselves as FBI agents

and asked to speak to the officer in charge. Barton was just outside the front door and knew they were feds as soon as he saw them walk up.

"Fucking feds!" he muttered to no one in particular.

Both Takoda and Mike were in the front of the house and heard him. They looked at each other and walked outside as Barton was walking up to the two men who immediately showed their fancy bifold wallets holding their badges and ID cards.

"Gentlemen! What can I do for the FBI?" Barton asked, knowing already there was about to be a hostile takeover.

Mike and Takoda made it right up behind Barton and stopped, the word the FBI was on scene spreading quickly through the search party.

"Good morning," the older agent began, "My name is Special Agent Forbes and this is Special Agent Sawyer. We are now looking into the killing of Janet Sweetwater and the related killing of the security guard. I hate to do it to you but you are a veteran, we're all professionals here, we are taking over as of now but by all means, go ahead and finish your search, book your evidence and file your reports. I don't want to be a dick or anything. But this case is under federal jurisdiction as of now."

"Is that right?" Barton said, shaking his head.

Mike couldn't be sure, but it seemed like Barton was more relieved to be out from under this joint investigation than he was angry about it being pulled from him.

"I take it you'll be wanting our stuff too?" Takoda said to the lead agent.

The agent looked Takoda and Mike up and down, lingering on Mike's name tag.

"You must be Armandarez of the Lakota Tribal Police?"

"Yup, that's me. I've met you before, about three years ago on the rez," Takoda said.

"That's right, I remember that," the agent said, "And you," he pointed a finger at Mike, "We've heard about you!" he smirked.

"Oh?" was all Mike could muster.

"We'll be in touch," Forbes said and turned and walked away with his partner.

"That's that then," Barton said, turning towards Takoda and wiping sweat from his forehead. "Nice working with ya," he said, then walked back into the house to break the news that everyone inside already knew.

Mike looked at Takoda.

"*Oh*! That's all you had to say to the guy, *Oh*!" Takoda said, smiling at him.

"He caught me off guard. They know about me? What does that even mean? And why are you smiling? I mean I know you always smile–it's your thing–but aren't you pissed?"

"It happens to us all the time," Takoda said.

Lodge Day

For two days now, the Loller brothers hid out in a cheap motel room, parking the Camaro in the back away from the street and the searching eyes of law enforcement. Troy had been in contact with his girlfriend who was freaking out about the whole situation, shocked that the two were wanted in connection with a murder. After all, they were supposed to be security for a big military contractor and were supposed to be the good guys...

The brothers argued. David didn't want to go back to prison. He would go out fighting, he told his brother, *suicide by cop* if he had to; he wasn't going back inside. He urged Troy to call the contact number for Blackrock Security and get advice on this situation, see if they could come and get them out of the area or something. All they had was a contact number. That's how Blackrock worked. A buddy at the range, another Marine, gave him the first phone number to call and then he was called back and given the job from another number. Blackrock wasn't listed in any phone directories. Money was deposited to his checking account twice a month from a numbered offshore account and that was that. This was an off-the-grid job for independent military contractors and Troy knew he had fucked up killing that damn Indian at L & M Logistics that night. Stupid fuck snooping inside where he wasn't supposed to be. He didn't even report that but they sure called him when they heard about it, said everything would be fine and gave him orders to terminate Janet Sweetwater quietly and unseen and then await further instructions. He didn't know what he'd done wrong? How did the cops even know about him? L & M were instructed not to acknowledge him or his brother as employees because, technically, they were not.

Their plan now, after plenty of arguments, was to ditch the Camaro near a rental place and rent a car; they would swing by the house late at night, get the girl, and leave town never to return. Troy was relieved when his phone rang and although it wasn't the normal number that was calling him, he was pretty sure it was Blackrock.

"Hello, who is this?" he asked.

"You know who this is," said a calm voice. "Now listen carefully if you two want to get out of this in one piece."

"You don't sound like the guy I contracted this gig with." Troy said skeptically.

"I'm not. I'm the extraction guy. You two need to get rid of that car you're driving. There is a want on that vehicle and warrants for both of you. We will change your names and get you new ID's when we take you in. Your girlfriend and child cannot come. Don't say goodbye to them and don't go back to the house: the FBI are now watching it

24/7. Are you with me so far, Marine?" the voice said with authority.

"Yes sir, did you serve?" Troy asked the voice, grasping at some sense of camaraderie in the midst of their desperate situation.

"No personal information soldier! Now get yourself and your coworker to the veteran's memorial on the rez at 2000 hours tonight. You will be contacted, sign/countersign is *Indian/Plunder.* Repeat that."

"I copy. *Indian/Plunder,* 2000 hours," Troy said, feeling much relieved to see a way out of their current predicament.

"Out." the voice said.

The call terminated.

"Was that Blackrock? Are we out of this dump?" David asked hopefully.

"Yes! I fucking told you, brother! Marines leave no man behind! I'm going to lose my girl and kid though..."

"It's okay bro," David said, jumping up off the bed and hugging his brother, "You can get another one! The important thing is we're out of here tonight!"

Mike's first RDO was routine. He did his obligatory morning workout and walked around the property with Max. The mornings were getting cold and autumn was upon them, winter just around the corner. But the Airstream had a good heater and he would buy some real winter clothing soon. Growing up in Southern California, Mike was out of his element in the South Dakota winter; fifty degrees felt cold to him. It meant an extra shirt under a light jacket. But he remembered going snow skiing as a kid up in Big Bear and Lake Arrowhead where he had his first experiences with snow and thermal underwear that his mom had bought him. Then there was Winter training in the Army and that was *really* cold. Mickey Mouse air filled boots and double layer wool/cotton Long Johns cold. He hated it. He was wishing right about now that he had kept those Army issue Long Johns and Parka.

Captain Trask came out after he got home from work and sat with Mike at the fire ring. They commiserated about the FBI taking over the case with Trask informing Mike that he had been put in for a commendation for procuring the joint investigation that had been fruitful, identifying the perpetrators and resulting in warrants, right up to the point the FBI snatched the glory away from them. The Sheriff himself was very happy with the investigation and received a call from the Director of Public Safety, his equal on the rez, thanking the Sheriff for their professionalism in the matter.

Mike said he didn't expect any awards or commendations, that he was just doing his job and shared his until-now unvoiced fears that many in the department were not too accepting of an outside officer coming in and rocking the boat, changing the status quo. Trask assured Mike that his presence was appreciated and reminded him that no matter how hard you try, you can't make everyone happy and that especially applies to cops.

After Trask left, Mike spent the rest of the day mentally preparing for tomorrow's lodge. He also started drinking a lot of water–he wanted to be fully hydrated before going in. The body sheds a lot of water in the lodge and being dehydrated going in had resulted in cramps and headaches in his past experiences. This was just one of hundreds of lessons he'd learned about the inipi ceremony. He went over what lodge was, what it meant to him as he sang songs in his head, practicing to remember the words.

Mike went over all his social media notifications one last time before going to bed. He always put his phone away on lodge day, not looking at any notifications in the morning except for his phone. If there was an important call or voicemail from work he would take it, but that was it. He needed to be in the proper state of mind to go into the womb of Mother Earth and pray. Before putting it down he noticed a new friend request on Facebook. He opened it up and it was Lucinda. She had found him on the popular social media app. He smiled at her profile picture and couldn't help but click on her profile and go through her *about* info and some of her photos. Wow, he thought, she was a lot thinner until recently. Perfect was the word that came to mind. His thumb hesitated over the accept button.

He didn't want to delete the request but he didn't want to accept it just yet…

Mike drove out onto the Reservation and retraced the path to Funmaker's place the best he could. The further out he got, the more unsure of himself he became, often stopping where two dirt roads intersected to look for recent tire tracks on the ground. He was getting a little frustrated with himself: he knew he was pretty darn good at land navigation and terrain orienteering in the military, but he didn't have a USGS Topographical map on him to read and he didn't think to drop a pin location on his cell phone last time he was here. He was glad to see a Jeep coming up behind him in his rear view mirror. He pulled off the dirt road to let it pass, hoping it was going to Funmaker's place.

The Jeep stopped as it came abreast of him and he could see Tully looking over at him questioningly.

"I'll follow you!" Mike shouted over the engine noise.

Tully just smiled and started out. Mike fell in behind him and much to his chagrin quickly learned that they were almost there. Had he gone up over one more rise in the road he would have seen the butte off to the right and the wash that led up to Funmaker's place with several tire tracks marking the turn off.

He shook his head. He just hadn't gone far enough. He

should have known. He knew from both police and military training that humans often don't go far enough when searching for something or retracing their steps, especially at night. But this being broad daylight, he was almost on top of Funmaker's place. They pulled in with four men, one being Funmaker and one other he recognized as Raymond Angry Boy, standing near the lodge grounds looking at them pull in, shaking his head. Mike just knew that Angry Boy was thinking that Mike was following Tully because he didn't know the way.

Great, he thought.

They parked next to the other vehicles and got out. Mike grabbed his bag that he had put tobacco in, along with several water bottles, a washcloth and towel and a change of clothing if needed. He also had a beaded turtle necklace a Lakota friend had made for him years ago that he always brought to lodge for good luck. He left his phone in his Tahoe.

"I had to rescue the wasicu," Tully said as they approached the men, who were waiting for them to arrive before entering the grounds all together.

They laughed, all but Angry Boy, who looked...angry.

"I almost made it," Mike said in his own defense.

"Kangee, washte lo," Funmaker said to Tully, then, "Mike, go smudge off and smudge everyone in."

"Yessir," Mike said as he smiled at the men, two of whom he did not know and Funmaker wasn't going to introduce, at least not at this point; introductions were more of a white man thing. He walked past them and into what would be considered the grounds area, setting down his bag and retrieving an abalone shell from next to the sacred mound just outside the east facing door of the Inipi. The shell had white sage in it in the form of a rolled up bundle, tied with red yarn. Mike lit the sage with his lighter, another part of his lodge day equipment, and then smudged himself, starting with his face and head, cupping and pulling the smoke with his free hand, then working his way down to his feet. He then walked around the grounds in a circle several times as he had been taught to do before coming back to the spot he had entered with the burning sage to assist each person upon entering the grounds.

The men came up to Mike, one at a time, and he handed them the burning sage. No words were needed. Each man had done this many times before. The two older men he didn't know, closer to Funmaker's age, came first. Then Funmaker and then Tully. Finally, Angry Boy came up to Mike and without eye contact accepted the sage, hesitating with his hand over the rising smoke of the sage to first smudge his hand before accepting it. Mike let the man do his thing, walking over to place the abalone shell next to the mound, then went to his bag and sat down where the other men were gathering.

Funmaker or one of the other men had already prepared the fire, the igneous stones stacked in the center of the logs, all coming to a peak like a wooden teepee. There were even some crumpled up newspapers in crevices at the base all set to be lit. The lodge itself was covered with tarps of various colors, underneath which Mike knew there were equally mismatched blankets. A five gallon bucket sat next to the front door flap, half full with water with a wooden ladle hanging inside.

"Mike, light the fire," Funmaker said.

"Yessir," he said, lit the fire, made sure it took, and then walked back over to the group.

"I have gifts, and a story to tell about them," Tully said.

Most of the men said something in pleasant surprise like, "Oh," or "A Ho," and sat down. Only Angry Boy and Funmaker remained standing.

Tully then began speaking in Lakota after telling Mike to follow along best he could.

"As you know, I go to inipi with Takoda at his place. I am happy to come sweat with Funmaker. It has been long since he held lodge, many years. It will be interesting to share with our new wasicu friend Mike Taylor; he has ... grown on me. He seems to know what he is doing. I can say this: at least he tries. So many of our people have lost their way spiritually or go to the Catholic church.

"I was driving down a dirt road on the rez last month praying to Tunkashila, telling him we are short on eagle feathers for the lodge. As I was driving along I saw a Golden Eagle swoop down in front of my Jeep and land in the field and fall over, dead. I stopped and walked over to the little brother and he was dead. Tunkashila answered my prayer right there on the spot. I took the bird in a good way and prepared it, taking every piece for our religious uses.

"Last week I passed out some of the feathers to those at our lodge that I knew needed them. I still have some and wanted to share with you here, to honor this new gathering, a new brother and old brothers that are coming back on the Red Road."

Tully opened his bag and took out a folded red cloth with several feathers gently held inside. As he unfolded the cloth Mike could see that these were indeed prized Golden Eagle wing feathers, all beaded expertly around the quill with four long leather tails coming off the ends. He then handed one each to the two older men sitting with him. They said "A Ho" in thanks for the spiritual gift. He then handed one to Funmaker who held it up and shook it reverently while making eye contact with Tully. He then handed one to Angry Boy who said, "A Ho, pelameyaya," in thanks for the gift.

Mike didn't think he was going to get one, and in all fairness he knew that he didn't deserve one, being new and wasicu. In fact, it was illegal for a non-Native to possess an eagle feather under federal law.

Tully then picked up the last feather and turned slightly towards Mike, who was sitting to his left, and handed it to him, much to his surprise.

"The spirits directed me to give one to you," he said.

"Wow! I don't know what to say! Peylameyaya, thank you!" he said.

"Jesus!" Angry boy said, shaking his head.

Everyone looked at Angry Boy in shock. He had pretty much ruined an otherwise good moment in time with his negative outburst, and using the name of the wasicu deity to boot. The smudging may have chased away any lingering evil spirits but it didn't have any effect on the man.

"You have a problem with my gift Raymond?" Tully asked.

"I have a problem with being here! Not with Lakota but with this wasicu! I don't know if I can sit next to a wasicu in lodge even, and you give him an eagle feather?"

"You can only be on one road, Ray, the Red Road or the Black Road. We've talked about this. Takoda says, like the old ones taught us, there is a time to step off the Red Road and paint our faces for war, but one must atone for this and step back onto the Red Road," Tully finished.

The older men nodded their heads in agreement with this and Rayond Angry Boy Whitecloud looked down at the ground, still angry.

"I have sweated with many men in my life," Funmaker began, weighing in for the first time, "Cheyenne brothers, Navajo, Crow, the Chumash from California, even rainbow lodges with the woman folk and children, cool lodges fully dressed with the lights on even, to share our ways. And I have sweated with a few wasicu in the past that came in a good way like this wasicu here. He is humble and he tries, like Kangee says. He built this lodge with me. We spoke long on what inipi is and he knows more than a lot of our own people. I am satisfied with him. I will sweat with him. If it matters who is sitting next to you in lodge then your faith is weak. No man, no matter where he is from or what color his skin is, should take you off your path."

Angry Boy continued looking down, deflated and humbled.

"I can tend the fire. I've tended fire before when some- one didn't want to sweat with me," Mike spoke up.

"Ssh!" Tully hushed him, then smiled.

"You will tend the fire," Funmaker said with a smile, and added, "but you are coming in too!"

The men were silent for a few moments when Funmaker said it was time to go in and smoke the pipe.

The men got undressed down to their underwear and walked to the door of the lodge where each one got down on their hands and knees and entered the womb of Mother Earth in a humble way. One of the older men turned and said something to Angry Boy. Mike couldn't hear it all– he was last in line and the man's Lakota was thick, but it sounded like he told Angry Boy to get right in the head or the stones would chase him out.

The men sat in a circle around the pit in the center of the sweat lodge where the stones would be placed. Mike was the last one in and sat next to the door flap so he could lift it after each round, go out and bring in more rocks.

Funmaker removed his sacred chanupa pipe from a handmade beaded bag and began loading it with the knick knick blend. He then lit the pipe and took several slow puffs before passing it around to each man who accepted it with reverence and went through their own ritual of where the pipe would touch their body, how they would smoke it and rotate it before passing it to the next man. This was an essential part of the inipi ceremony, undertaken so there would be no lies between them. Mike accepted his turn and smoked the chanupa as he had done many times before, his first time being when he was ten years old. Funmaker took the chanupa when it came back to him and handed it back to Mike along with the bag and told Mike to bring in four stones.

Mike went out and placed the chanupa on top of its bag on the sacred mound. He then went to the fire, which had now burned down to hot coals exposing the top rocks. He used the sticks and deer antlers to manipulate the rocks. It was hot and he missed using a shovel. He retrieved them one at a time and used a well-burnt whisk broom to dust off ash and debris before taking them in and putting them in the pit. Funmaker placed some sage and sweetgrass on the red hot rocks, igniting the dried herbs and giving off a pleasant-smelling smoke.

When all the rocks were brought in for the first round

Mike came in after loosening the flap behind him. He pulled it in tight around the bottom making sure no outside light came in before taking his seat. He felt the temperature going up in the lodge, smelled the earth and the wood of the lodge itself along with the sweetgrass and sage. It was like coming home, he thought, enjoying these senses, seeing the men sitting around him in the dull red glow of the lava rocks, well suited to the purpose they were being put to. He knew though that the pain and heat were coming.

Funmaker began the first round, telling them the purpose and the subject of this round and each man prayed out loud, one at a time, going in the same direction as the chanupa. They either prayed out loud or in silence. Most did pray audibly, but Angry Boy said he would pray in silence and then Tully did as well. When it finally got back to Funmaker, Mike knew he would pour the water.

He heard Funmaker getting some water and was ready for the heat as it hit the stones with a splash and an intense sizzling sound. The water was immediately vaporized on contact into scalding hot steam with no place to go. More splashing and sizzling followed as the red glow was extinguished into darkness and men grunted in pain. It was so hot it hurt to breathe; even Mike's fingers felt as if they were on fire as he held his little washcloth to his face to breathe through. This was cheating, he knew, but he had to do it. It was probably the hottest first round he had ever experienced in his life.

Finally, after several agonizing moments that felt like minutes, Funmaker said to open the flap. Mike didn't have to be told twice as he scrambled out, pushing the flap outwards, got up and fixed it open and sat down just outside to listen for instructions to bring in the next stones. He could see most of the faces inside, now covered with sweat. He noted that Angry Boy looked a bit distressed. Everyone said they were alright and they proceeded with the second round, repeating the steps of the first with different intentions for this round, different prayers and a song by Funmaker on his hand drum before he again poured the water. Mike concentrated on his prayers to get him through the pain, held his cheater rag to his face waiting, just waiting for the order to throw open the flap again when someone brushed past him and the flap pushed open. Someone couldn't take the heat and rushed out.

Funmaker said to open the flap and Mike went out to find Angry Boy lying on the ground in a sweaty heap next to his clothes, breathing hard and moaning in distress. After fixing the flap, Mike went over and asked him if he was okay. He did not answer.

Mike grabbed two water bottles out of his own bag and poured one over Angry Boy's face and upper body. The young man grunted at the cool water and opened his eyes. Mike bent down and placed the other water bottle in his hand and told him to drink some water and sit up when he could. Angry Boy just nodded.

The men inside could hear what was going on outside, heard Mike's words. They didn't say a thing. They had all seen grown men run out of lodge before, experienced men that for whatever reason had to go. Sometimes men scrambled right over the rocks or the other men in their haste for fresh air and relief. Men had been known to go right under the ribs of the lodge to get out if they had to. It was not considered a disgrace. There was always a reason. It was more important to learn from the experience.

Lodge went on for two more rounds, until Funmaker signaled the end of lodge by saying, "And all the people said..." to which everyone answered, "Mitakuye oyasin," in response, to honor all their ancestors and family.

Mike checked on the younger man each time he came out. The last time Mike saw that the second water bottle was empty and Angry Boy was gone. He looked over at the cars and could see the back door of the man's Chevy Monte Carlo was open, a head lying back in the seat.

It had been a short first lodge with only six participants, five for the last two rounds, only taking a little over two hours. But it was quality. Mike's legs were a bit wobbly and he was covered with sweat, his white skin mottled red in splotches.

"Look, we burned the wasicu! He looks like a lobster!" one of the older men said upon exiting the lodge and seeing Mike's skin.

As the others exited the inipi they looked at Mike's skin

and all commented on it. He held his arms out and checked out his own torso and legs and he was indeed burnt in odd patterns of red on white flesh. It felt like sunburn.

"I had a pinto pony that color once," Tully said, which garnered a few laughs.

The men dried themselves off, stood and air-dried for a while, some drinking water as Mike did himself, downing three bottles in a row, before grabbing his last water bottle to give to Angry Boy. He walked over and found the younger man asleep. Mike gently placed the water bottle between the man's legs.

The men dressed and talked a bit, not much. They may have come out of the womb a new man, to live again, but they were spent physically and emotionally if they did it right. The four directions, the four peoples, the four elements and the four colors of the Lakota medicine wheel had been touched. It was much to reflect on and the men were still within themselves in their thoughts as it should be.

Mike dried off and dressed himself. He wanted to go home and take a long shower and sleep. It had been a good day. He decided he would be first to leave, let the true Natives talk about him. He figured they wanted to let Raymond Angry Boy recover. The rocks had indeed chased him out for whatever reason–he suspected it was due to the man's state of mind while inside the lodge. He had to come back tomorrow and help Funmaker take down and fold the tarps and blankets after letting them dry, clean up the grounds and all, so he said goodbye to all, shaking hands with Funmaker last. He then got in his Tahoe and left.

As soon as he drove away Angry Boy scrambled out of his back seat holding the water bottle Mike had given him. There was a look of panic on his face. He looked at the water bottle, knowing Mike had put it in his hand and looked at the men, now looking at him in curiosity.

"Was that Taylor? We have to stop him!" he shouted as he began jogging towards them.

He made it three quarters of the way to them and stumbled to the ground.

"Are you alright Raymond?" Tully asked, stepping towards him.

"You don't understand! I was supposed to stab him! They're going to shoot him if he leaves here before me!" he blurted out, looking up at Tully.

"What the fuck? Are you serious Raymond? What have you done?" Tully asked.

"Stop him!" Raymond said, rolling over onto his back, shading his eyes from the sun with his forearm.

Tully looked back at the three older men. There was real concern on their faces. They knew this was a bad wind, knew what would happen if a white law enforcement officer was shot on the rez...again.

Funmaker motioned for Tully to go.

Tully ran back and grabbed his bag before running for his Jeep, fishing for his keys in the bottom of his bag.

Sicaiah

Mike turned off the trail leading down from Funmakers place and started along the long dusty road that would take him into the rez proper where he could find his way out. He'd been driving for about five minutes when he saw Tully's Jeep at a distance, come flying up the road behind him, leaving a plume of dust. He thought maybe he'd forgotten something–he couldn't figure out why the big man would be driving so fast. Mike slowed for a little gully that crossed the road, going through one of dozens of washes that crossed it. He had to negotiate to the right and over some rough stuff at the bottom before heading up the other side. He saw a flat spot just up ahead and pulled over to the right, next to the lip of the wash that now ran along the road.

Mike thought he saw movement down in the wash behind him and pushed himself up using the brake as a step and leaned to his right to get a closer look in his rearview mirror when his rear window shattered with a pop followed by a pinch in his left shoulder that felt like a bee sting. His front window cracked. He looked forward at his windshield in shock and saw a small lead bullet, a .22 Long Rifle from the look of it, lying on the dash.

I've been shot! He realized, and punched it. But he pulled the wheel to the right in haste and his Tahoe launched right into the wash, hitting the bottom with a bone-jarring thud before landing on its rear wheels, wedging the vehicle inside a rut. He got out quickly and grabbed his bag, fumbling for his Glock and fell over backwards on the ground as he pulled the gun clear and began scanning for the shooter. He knew the shooter was behind him and Tully should be up to him soon too. For a split second he thought Tully shot him but that didn't make sense, he just sweated with the man, and somebody was in the wash.

Someone was walking up the wash from the direction of the gully where he had crossed. Mike could hear them and see their feet approaching under his Tahoe–two men. He waited from his lying position and raised his Glock to shoot as soon as the assailants, whoever they were, cleared the back of his Tahoe. A seventeen-year-old Native American he recognized as one of Angry Boy's friends came around the back of the SUV first, holding a rifle and looking inside the Tahoe.

"Hurry up! There's another car coming!" said the man behind him.

"It's probably Ray! Shut up! I got the wasicu, I saw him flinch!" the boy said confidently. In truth it had been a hell of a shot. Had Mike not raised up and to his right in his seat the round would have hit him right in the base of his skull.

"Drop the rifle!" Mike said, pointing his Glock directly at the young man.

They had been looking for Mike to be dead inside the SUV. They didn't expect him to be lying on the ground in the rut just past the vehicle, armed and taking aim at them. The only reason Mike didn't shoot immediately was because he knew the boy was, well, a boy.

Shocked, the boy looked over at Mike and the barrel of his gun pointed directly at him and quickly dropped the .22 rifle in the dirt.

"What the fuck did you two just do?" came Tully's booming voice from the lip of the wash above them.

Mike turned his head only slightly, keeping his target within his peripheral vision, to see Tully standing on the lip, dust drifting past him from quickly sliding to a stop and alighting from his vehicle.

"Finishing the job Ray was supposed to do!" the youngster said.

"Yeah, *Ray* changed his mind on the whole stabbing plan! You two are going to jail! Mike, are you good?" Tully asked.

"I'm hit. Shoulder somewhere, through and through," Mike said as he got up, picked up his bag and began walking towards the two young men. "Start walking, back the way you came and up to Officer Brown's Jeep!"

"*Officer Brown,* as if! He's Kangee to us, white man!" the older one said, then added, "We sweat with him!"

"Get moving!" Mike ordered as the two began walking back towards the gully where they could walk up onto the road. Mike retrieved his phone from the floorboard of the passenger seat but left the keys in the ignition. Whoever came to get it would need them. A tow truck with a winch was definitely needed.

"It's Officer Brown today, you two boneheads!" Tully said as the two approached him behind his Jeep, "Do you know what happened the last time a white cop was shot on this reservation? You don't because you were too young! Cops, Feds, all up our asses! Hands on the Jeep, I gotta pat you down!"

Tully frisked them for weapons and told them to sit down. Then he turned to Mike, who was putting his glock back in his bag; he was wincing at the pain in his left shoulder.

"How bad is it? Let me see," he said, moving forward to inspect the wound.

"I'm not bleeding, so that's a good sign. Ten years in the ghetto and a tour in the sandbox without a scratch and I get shot on an Indian reservation!" he said angrily. It was the first time Tully had seen Mike lose his temper or use the word *Indian*. He was usually very respectful, using the terms *Native American* and *First Nations*. Guess he was human after all, Tully thought as he looked at Mike's trapezius, pulling his T-shirt back on both sides.

"Through and through, muscle of the trap. You will need an x-ray to make sure it didn't hit anything important like nerve or bone. You got lucky!"

Funmaker's truck was coming up the road now with someone in the passenger seat. It was Angry Boy.

"So, what was this *plan* Raymond had?" Mike asked.

"Apparently Ray was going to stab you at lodge and if you left first these two were going to be the backup plan! Fucking geniuses!" Tully said, "I'm gonna book all three of them! Funmaker can get you to the Indian clinic, it's closest and the doc was a combat surgeon."

"What the fuck? I come here in a good way to sweat! Probably going to get fired too? They fucking told me not to go on the reservation!"

Funmaker pulled up slowly and stopped. He said something to Angry Boy who nodded and slouched down in the cab of the truck and began staring off into the distance. Funmaker got out and walked right up to the two young men sitting on the ground and looked down at them, shaking his head. They did not look up at him. He then looked over at Mike's Tahoe down in the wash before coming back to Mike and Tully, asking what happened.

Mike told him what had happened and Tully took over, finally saying he was going to charge all three of them.

"Mmmm, this is going to be bad," Funmaker said, knowing the news would get out. Feds, State Police, and the Sheriff's Department would all be called in. All the good that Mike had done bringing the two departments and cultures closer together with the hope of future cooperation would be destroyed because of the actions of a few immature Native American men wanting to make their bones, garnering some respect from those that followed the Movement against white government.

It was as if Mike was reading the old man's mind. Just the presence of Funmaker had calmed him and although his shoulder was hurting more by the minute, he knew this all rested on him. After all, his presence had been the catalyst in this action...

"Fuck it," Mike began, walking over to the two, "You two need to be more careful in the future when conducting target practice on the rez! Shooting at bottles and cans is fine if you clean up your mess and always, always make sure your backdrop is clear!"

The two looked up at Mike in shock. Was the wasicu really giving them a way out of this?

Tully looked on in surprise too. Only Funmaker seemed to understand what Mike was doing, a stony look on his face.

"Mike, are you sure you want to do this? They tried to kill you! You sweated with that moron!" Tully said, turning and pointing at Angry Boy in the cab of the truck, trying to listen through the open windows, "and he came with ill intent! No wonder the rocks chased you out!"

"The black road," Mike said as he dropped his bag. He was losing feeling in his hand. He bent forward and grabbed his shoulder as a sharp pain hit, "Ah, fuck!"

"Kangee!" Funmaker said, "Take him in. I'll take these two. We're going to have a long talk. Call Takoda too!"

"You heard him, get up! Today is your lucky day! Come on Mike," Tully said, picking up Mike's bag and helping him in the passenger seat of his Jeep.

It was a bumpy ride to the Indian Clinic, Tully driving faster then he needed to. Twice Mike asked him to slow down and twice he did slow down–momentarily. Tully parked in the fire lane in front of the door marked Urgent Care and helped Mike in, opening the door for him.

"We got a gunshot wound here!" Tully announced with his big voice, causing everyone inside to stop talking and look up. There were only a few patients, mostly colds and flu, on this side of the clinic. Most patients were on the other side waiting for routine appointments. Staff outnumbered patients on this side on a Wednesday afternoon.

"We don't normally treat gunshot wounds here," a receptionist said, "this is urgent care, not a trauma center. You can take him to County or we can call paramedics!"

"Police emergency! Tell Doc Weller that Officer Brown is here with a wounded officer! Do it now!"

The receptionist disappeared to the back as Tully took Mike up to the counter to start filling out forms. Mike was okay under his own power but he really wanted something for the pain right about now...

A nurse came out of the entry door to the inner clinic

and recognized Tully and Mike immediately. They knew her too.

"What the hell happened?" Star Wichahpi Whitecloud asked, standing there in her blue scrubs, ID with a big *RN* in red letters hanging from her breast pocket.

Tully of course knew she worked there; Mike had no idea.

"Ask your brother and his two bonehead friends! Sergeant Taylor has a through and through to his trapezius area, just need an x-ray and a penicillin shot and he'll be fine. He's a combat vet."

Star walked quickly towards the two men.

"What the fuck are you talking about? *My brother and his friends?"* she whispered, "Did Raymond shoot you?" she asked with a look of extreme concern on her face.

"It was an accident," Mike said, admiring just how good she looked in a nurse's uniform, scrubs or not. He was in pain but just couldn't help himself.

Tully just shook his head.

Star was confused, looking back and forth at Tully and Mike before making a split decision.

"Follow me!" she said, turning on her heel and opening the door with a key card.

She took them back to an empty exam room right next to the doctor's office where he could be heard calling in a prescription for a patient.

"Doc, I need you! GSW!" she yelled as she passed.

Mike was happy to sit down on the exam table, a gurney, as Star began taking off his shirt. She looked at the wound on both sides and grabbed a blood pressure cuff, started to get his vitals to begin a chart on him. Tully excused himself to go get those forms in the lobby and to make a few phone calls, leaving Mike in Star's capable hands.

She asked Mike what happened and he told her it was just a big mistake: target practice gone wrong, just friends out shooting at cans and didn't see him. She looked at him skeptically.

"Shooting cans? My brother was out shooting cans?"

"Americans," Mike said and laughed.

All expression left her face and for a moment the beautiful dark skin of her face seemed to pale.

"What have we got here?" Doctor Weller said, coming into the room.

Star took a deep breath to compose herself before turning to the doctor.

"Sergeant Mike Taylor of the Sheriff's Department was shot through and through to the upper trapezius area, minimal bleeding, he is stable and alert, ambulatory, with Officer Tulliver Brown bringing him in."

The doctor looked at Mike and immediately examined the wound, putting on latex gloves. He was in his fifties and wore a white lab coat over the same brand of blue scrubs that Star and the other nurses wore.

"You know I have to report all gunshot wounds,

no matter how minor, but since you are a cop and Tully brought you in I reckon that's already done. Tell me what happened while I irrigate this wound and numb it up. Star, can you get me the portable, 2 cc's of lidocaine, 2%, a 10 cc with a 16 gauge needle, a 1cc and we'll go from there. I don't normally treat GSW's here, but if Tully brought you in... How are you doing?"

Star left to get the portable x-ray machine and the other supplies plus the saline she knew the doctor would need for irrigation, and a suture kit just in case.

"Just some boys shooting .22's and didn't see me down-range is all. No big deal."

"You're not in shock, so I know that's gotta sting a bit. Were you military?"

"Yessir. Army, one tour but no injuries."

"Me too, Army," the doc smiled, "Lead or copper jacket on the projectile, do you know?"

"Lead, 22 Long Rifle."

"Mmm, okay. Hopefully all it hit was soft tissue. Luckily it was a small bore. You will be off work for a while. It's going to really hurt and stiffen up tomorrow."

Star came back and dropped supplies on the foot of the gurney and left again, all professional now. She didn't even look at him. The doctor started numbing the area and then began irrigating the wound. Mike didn't look. The saline running down his back and chest was cold, but he was just glad to be numbed up. Tully returned with paperwork and said he called it in to TP, but not his department. That he could do that after he was home. The x-ray was okay, no bones hit and no remaining lead in the wound. The doctor gave Mike a big shot in the hip of some heavy duty antibiotic and wrote him a script for Amoxicillin and told him to follow up with his own physician in a week, but if he had any complications–fever or infected discharge–to go to the closest urgent care. He left the wound open to drain, putting a dressing on both sides, and said it was small enough to close on its own. He asked Mike if he wanted something for pain and Mike decided to be macho in front of Star and Tully, declining, saying he had Motrin and Tylenol at his trailer.

The doctor left and Tully followed him to his office, leaving Mike alone with Star who had begun cleaning up.

"I don't know what really happened out there, but I will find out!" she said, "I think you're covering something up and Tully is in on it too. I don't know if I should thank you or smack you. You really smell like a locker room by the way."

"We were at lodge, me and Tully, Raymond too, well, for two rounds anyway."

"Raymond left lodge early?" she asked incredulously, "Wait, he sweats on Sunday with Takoda?"

"He had an issue today and we were at Funmaker's place."

"Old Funmaker? He quit holding lodge before I was

born! Something to do with his son leaving the rez. That's crazy."

"Yeah, he came out to my trailer and asked me to build a lodge with him and start sweating. I think Hobby was behind it. He likes to meddle, you know. He even suggested I ask out Lucinda but Tully was against it. I was kind of thinking of asking you out…" he stalled.

Her demeanor became defensive.

"I would say no. If you think my brother and his stupid friends are bad, you should meet my uncles! It would never work but I am flattered. You are an … interesting guy Mike. You should ask her out. She talks about you all the time."

Star helped him with his T-shirt and helped him up. His arm was getting stiff. She gave him a military-like simple sling and fitted it around his right shoulder and helped him place his left arm in it. He was really wishing he'd taken the pain shot right about now as he knew it was really going to hurt when the lidocaine wore off. They walked to the doctor's office where Tully stood, talking to the doctor.

"You ready to go?" Tully asked him.

"Yup, let's roll partner," Mike said, acting brave for Star and the doc.

"Oh brother," she said, "I will be talking to you, both of you, soon!"

They drove to Captain Trask's house with Mike directing him the last part of the way and along the side of the house. Apparently Hobby had given Tully the approximate location of Mike's Airstream in previous conversations–of course he had. Tully had to get out and open the gate, and Max came running across the property from the direction of the firepit, head high, tail wagging.

"That your dog? I thought it was a coyote," Tully said.

"Yup, Australian Cattle Dog. He's my pal."

"What a fucking day, huh? Sicaiah! (Cursing)" Tully said.

"Sicaiah," Mike repeated.

Tully helped Mike out, opening the door for him and opening the Airstream door for him as well. He told Tully he was fine even though the lidocaine was wearing off and he was going to double medicate with Tylenol and Motrin as soon as he left. Tully said he would call him in a few hours as soon as he got back out to Funmaker's to see what was happening with his Tahoe and the three youngsters.

As soon as he left, Mike did just that, swallowing some pills and cracking open a beer to wash it down. He knew he would be stiff soon and needed to think about what happened today and what it meant going forward, not to mention what his work was going to do when he told them he had been accidentally shot on the reservation… But, Star's words about him stinking echoed in his ears so he got himself undressed and ran the shower. He didn't care if the bandages got wet: he had plenty of first aid kits lying around to dress the wounds.

The shower felt good, when the water wasn't falling

directly on his left trap. He stood under the showerhead for a long time till the water started to turn cool, knowing he'd used up the contents of his small water heater. He slowly and gingerly dried off and put on some comfortable sweats and sat down on the couch to surf the internet. He was soon sound asleep on his right side, the exhaustion of the Inipi ceremony taking over as the adrenaline of the shooting wore off. It was nighttime when he heard Max barking in his dream. As he woke, he realized Max was barking in the real world that was now completely dark. He heard a truck slowly pulling up next to the trailer. He tried to push himself up but could not. He was too sore to move. He just listened to the sound of a hydraulic ramp lowering, and chains being unfastened and knew from hearing those exact sounds hundreds of times that a flatbed tow truck was outside lowering a vehicle to the ground. He knew it was someone bringing his Tahoe home. He waited for them to knock but they never did. Instead, the truck slowly drove away and down the dirt road. He listened till he could no longer hear it and went back to sleep.

Lucinda

At 8 pm, the Loller brothers pulled into the Oglala Lakota-Dakota-Nakota Nation's US Veterans memorial, just off of a rural county road. It had been built here so Native American and Non-Native alike could visit and share the memorial. It consisted of a round concrete platform ringed with plinths, on each a plaque memorializing a conflict fought by Native Americans. A visitor could read them while gazing out at the surrounding natural land of the indigenous peoples of this area.

The parking lot was a simple one with only one other car, an older dark blue Chevy Suburban backed into a parking stall right in front of the memorial. A lone occupant in the driver's seat, smoking a cigarette. Troy decided that, just to be sure and show his tactical worth to the Blackrock representative extracting them, he would park his car facing the other vehicle with his lights on and they would approach on foot from behind their lights, guns not drawn but in their belts and at the ready. When he got close enough, he would utter the sign and wait for the countersign. He wanted to show the representative that they were professionals and could be counted on to be used on more jobs.

David didn't have the military training his Marine Corps brother had, so he followed his lead in matters like this.

The two wanted men got out and walked slowly to the Suburban.

They didn't make it.

As soon as they'd finished parking, two Native American men in dark clothing got ready to move from their position of concealment in the brush just past the far side of the parking lot. When the brothers Loller got out and began moving forward, so did the other two men, each creeping up quickly behind the brothers in soft-soled tra-ditional shoes that made little noise–nothing that could be heard over the idling engine noise of the Camaro and the Suburban that had also been left intentionally running.

The man in the Suburban just sat and smoked, blowing distracting plumes out the opened window. The brothers keyed on the glow of the cigarette, the exhale of smoke. They weren't expecting anything other than what was hap-pening right in front of them.

The driver watched the brothers as they cleared the Camaro and came into the light, one on each side, backlit and appearing as black silhouettes. It was a good approach, the driver had to admit. He watched two more figures come up swiftly and strike the men down with one blow each to the back of the head, knowing right where to strike to cause a quick and easy knockout using a soft leather sap filled with powdered lead. One man still moved on the ground and was struck a second time just behind the ear. The men went to Troy, picked him up and carried him to the back of the Suburban where the smoking man had gotten out and lifted the back hatch. They zip-tied Troy's hands behind his back and placed a cloth potato sack over his head and then went for David. Both were secured and left lying in the back as the men got in and drove off, leaving the Camaro idling, doors open, a Flying Dutchman left on the South Dakota plains.

Mike woke to the sound of Max growling at an approaching car. He realized it was morning and he badly needed to pee. He tried to right himself and could not: all the Motrin and Advil had worn off and it was just too painful to move. He listened to the car and decided it was a small one based on the engine noise. It sounded tinny and hollow like one of the Korean autos. He heard one door open and the rustling of plastic. He had to wonder if someone was bringing him groceries.

There came a knock at the door, soft, like a girl's knock.

Max barked once, that sharp, high-pitched yip of his breed.

"Max! Cool it!" He said.

"Mike, can I come in?" came a concerned female voice through the door.

He recognized the voice as Lucinda's almost immediately, even though it was a bit muffled from the barrier between them.

"It's unlocked! I … can't get up! Could use some help actually," he said, mostly to himself.

Lucinda opened the door slowly, looking at Max first, wagging his tail now, then over at Mike lying on his side on the couch. Mike could smell bacon and knew the white plastic bags she was carrying had food in them. He was suddenly famished, but first things first: he needed to right himself and he needed to use the latrine.

"You can't get up?" she echoed.

"I just need a hand, been here all night. The Tylenol has worn off. Hey, how'd you know where I live?"

Lucinda set the bags down on the kitchen table and patted Max on the head. The dog was already sniffing at the food as he hadn't eaten yet either. She walked up to him and bent over, placing a hand under Mike's neck. He got a full view of her lovely cleavage right in front of his face that no matter how hard he tried to ignore, there it was. Her full hips and the soft scent of a really lovely perfume were almost more enticing than the smell of the food.

"How do you think?" she asked rhetorically as she started to lift him. "Hobart War Club, more knowledgeable than rez radio! I called him last night after Star called me and said you got shot! I can't believe that! She told me it wasn't bad but that I should check up on you. She said you mentioned me at the clinic?"

Mike could hear the hopefulness and concern in her voice. Even though he was in excruciating pain as she lifted him up into a sitting position, he could feel the emotions in her voice while at the same time trying to sit up and not scream like a baby.

That little sneak! He thought. Star was practically throwing Lucinda at him.

He took several short breaths as his left shoulder settled.

"Can you help me stand up? I need to visit the facilities. How do you know Star by the way? From the restaurant?" he asked, abruptly changing the subject.

He gave her his right hand and she gently pulled him forward as he stood up.

"We went to High School together, and we are a small tribe. More than half of enrolled members live off the rez so those of us that live *on* the rez are pretty tight; even though she is traditional and I am Catholic, we're redskins first," she chuckled nervously.

"So you decided to bring me breakfast? You are the best! I'm starving!" he said as he walked gently to the bathroom, "But, who is manning the front counter of the Thunderbird?"

"I work in the afternoons and I only work to help out; I go back to school soon. I wanted to hear from you what happened."

Mike got into the small quarters of the Airstream bathroom and realized he didn't want to stand and pee and have Lucinda hear him right before they were going to eat together–well, he assumed she was going to eat too… So, he tested his shoulder, turning side to side, too and fro and started to bend forward to pull his sweats down. It hurt. He could only get them down a little of the way, enough to sit. He decided to brush his teeth for good measure and took some pills before going back out to his angel of the morning, who was really growing on him by the moment. It was a little after 8 am. She had gotten up really early to doll herself up and go get them breakfast. She was a very thoughtful person, he realized.

When he went back out front, Lucinda was pulling styrofoam boxes, big and small, out of the bag. Again he smelled the food and her perfume and couldn't decide which smelled better. He went to the kitchen and opened a cabinet off to one side to get Max's dry food. He had to take a knee to get into the bag and get the dog a scoop from the big plastic coffee cup he used to measure out Max's meals (when he got dry food), and went to his bowl. Lucinda met him and took the cup and poured it.

"You're doing too much! Sit! Eat!" she commanded softly.

He sat down and let her place a container in front of him. As she did so she turned her face towards him and kissed him, her soft warm lips parting and just a bit of tongue touching his lips, threatening ever so gently to part them.

Mike's eyebrows shot up in surprise as a warm glow began to spread all over his body, starting with his face. Suddenly his trapezius didn't feel so bad.

"What was that for?" he asked.

"I don't know? I just wanted to kiss you," she answered.

"Do you always kiss your boyfriends first?"

"No! I've never had a boyfriend before so… I've just wanted to kiss you ever since the first time I saw you. Is that what you are now, my boyfriend?" she asked, coming out of her momentary defensive shyness at his question.

"Kiss me again," Mike suggested.

She leaned over and kissed him again, this time he was ready for it, eagerly letting his lips part with hers, accepting her warm tongue into his mouth. He touched her tongue with his own, let them commingle lovingly, almost erotically for a moment before she pulled back, nibbling his lower lip as she straightened up and sat down.

"Eat! Your eggs are getting cold!" she smiled, looking down.

"Wow," was all he said, looking at her beauty as if for the first time before looking down himself and starting to eat, the warm glow now completely engulfing him. He didn't know why but he got the image of the Grinch in his mind from the old original Christmas cartoon with Boris Karloff as the narrator, right at the part where the Grinch's heart grew two sizes.

"Maybe you could accept my Facebook request?" she said shyly.

"Maybe I should!" he said and they laughed, then settled into eating in silence for a time.

After a while, Mike trying to eat slowly and with his mouth shut, he felt the silence was getting a bit too loud and awkward. He began to tell her what happened, starting with lodge and going through the shooting and then the visit to the clinic and for some reason, perhaps due to what had just transpired between them, he told her the truth. He said Star suspected as much but this needed to remain between them: the official story that it had been an accident had to be the only one told about the matter or heads would roll, the tribe would suffer.

Lucinda stopped eating at the point where Mike was shot and drove into the wash, her lovely brown face paleing a bit, her big brown eyes filling with tears as she listened intently. She grabbed a napkin and dabbed at her eyes and again looked down at her lap for a time until he finished his story.

"So, what happens now?" she asked him.

"Well, If I don't get fired you mean? I guess I call work today and tell them. I'm going to be on the desk for a while. Tully took care of the report on the rez so everything jibes. But cops aren't stupid. They will suspect something happened and I was told to stay off the rez but they were talking about on duty...I think? How is it that a beautiful girl like you has never had a boyfriend at 22 years old, by the way?"

"I just love school and learning. For me it was an escape from the reservation, people hating on the white man and his government all the time. Learning takes my mind off those negative thoughts. Star's uncles, brothers, all part of the movement. My parents taught me not to hate. I mean what makes us any different than the white man that hates us for the color of our skin if we do the same in return? Right? The bible tells us not to hate, and not to visit the sins of the father on the son. You were a soldier. You fought right alongside other soldiers that were from the First Nations, right? You weren't one of the 7th Cav that gunned down over 300 Lakota men, women and children at Wounded Knee. It is all frustrating so I just study, concentrate on that. I never had time for a boyfriend."

"That's a lot to take in. Wow. But you have time for a boyfriend now? And a white boyfriend? You are going to be a scandal!" he said jokingly.

"Yeah, I guess so," she smiled, "Besides, you are different. You're like a Lakota in a white body. Here I'm the Indian and I'm Catholic, but you are the one going to inipi? My parents are going to flip out!"

"You're just about to go back to school so what, I only get to see you on weekends? Oh, I have to talk to Tully about this too. He didn't want me to ask you out when Hobby suggested it. He believes whites should be with whites but not for the reasons you might think, at least what I thought. He says he's not too prejudice, he just believes

Native Americans have a duty to populate a dwindling race. That's how he explained it to me anyways," Mike said.

"Oh, I didn't know that. He's hard to read. If he talks to you at all he must like you. He doesn't talk to a lot of Indians even. I will be home weekends and holidays and maybe you can come up during the week on your days off from time to time. I can show you around? There are a lot of great little bars and restaurants around the college, or maybe I'll just come home and commute?" she mused.

"Hey, we just kissed, twice and they were great kisses, fantastic! But, we are just starting out so you don't change anything and we can go slow. I don't want to screw this up like I have in the past. Slow is good, okay?" he asked her.

She gave him a funny look like she wanted to hear more about that last part but she didn't pry.

They finished eating and Lucinda cleared everything, placing it back in the plastic bags. Mike suggested they go for a walk around the property so he could loosen up his shoulder, see how bad it was, and walk Max.

After an hour or more of walking around the property several times, having one of those *getting to know you* talks during which they talked about many things from her family members, likes and hobbies to his. She asked him why he lived in a trailer, even though it was a really nice one, why he broke up with his last girlfriend, and about quitting in Santa Ana and moving here. He told her he liked living outdoors away from the city lights where he could hike, see the stars at night. He also told her that he wanted kids someday but his ex, whom he'd dated for three years, lived with for one, didn't want to *ruin her body* with pregnancies and was a city girl, born and raised. Other than a few Mexican dishes her mother taught her to cook, the only thing she ever made for dinner were reservations. When they decided to go their separate ways he still had to hear her voice on the radio and see her in the halls. That and not being promoted to sergeant just because he was branded a loner for not going to all the police parties and for practicing Lakota spirituality led to his decision to leave.

They were so enamored with each other that this talk could have gone on for hours, probably would have, until a county black & white came up the dirt road and turned onto Trask's property. They were almost back to the Airstream on one of their laps. Mike noted the Ford SUV was new, an Expedition perhaps. When Captain Trask got out of the passenger seat to open his own gate Mike realized this was the brass–the big brass.

"Oh crap!" he said.

"What? What is it?" Lucinda asked.

"I think that's the Sheriff. I haven't even met him yet! They must know. My ass is grass!"

She grabbed his hand to calm him and together they walked hand in hand to the front of the trailer as the big SUV came up and stopped, the driver in uniform complete with RayBan sunglasses, a tan cowboy hat and five shiny gold stars on each collar. The captain pointed at Mike's wrecked Tahoe with shattered rear window and said something to the Sheriff who just nodded.

Mike stood with Lucinda and tried to smile and look natural. His heart was pounding.

Sheriff Buck Tillerman

Troy Loller woke to the smell of dirt and the rocking of a vehicle on an uneven road. His hands were tied behind his back and there was something covering his head as he lay prone. He felt a body next to him and knew instinctively that it was his brother. He could hear talking coming from the front of the vehicle, something about a white police officer one of them was vouching for, to the objection of at least two other voices.

He had a splitting headache and was a bit dizzy. He knew he was concussed. It was still dark so he figured he hadn't been out that long and tried to piece together what had happened. It took a few minutes of fighting through the fog to come to the mistaken realization that he had been set up by the folks at Blackrock Security. What he couldn't figure out was why they were using Native Americans to kidnap them. He nudged his brother but he didn't stir. He was worried about him but his body was warm and he didn't feel dead: that was a good sign.

He tried to listen to the Indians in the front; they were all talking and laughing like it was just another day on the rez. The one voice that had been saying the white cop was a good guy and that not all whites were bad, was now saying something about a red road and a black road, whatever that was, and that it was important to regain balance. There were a lot of foreign words mixed in so he couldn't follow very well. One thing was for sure: Troy and his brother were in trouble. He needed to come up with a plan and wait for a moment, the right moment, to get them out of this situation.

The sheriff looked over at Mike and Lucinda, standing there holding hands, with no expression on his face. He looked them up and down momentarily and cut the engine. The first thing Mike saw coming out of the SUV as the Sheriff opened the door was a perfectly shined pair of black Wellington cowboy boots.

Mike took a deep breath. Lucinda squeezed his hand then let go of it. She said she was going to go clean up and went up into the trailer, leaving the door open.

Captain Trask came around from the passenger side and up next to the Sheriff, who was now regarding his new Deputy Sergeant.

"Sheriff Tillerman! It's a pleasure to finally meet you. Captain Trask, I needed to talk to you actually…" he fumbled.

"We need to talk, *sergeant,*" the Sheriff said.

Mike looked at Captain Trask, who he now considered a friend, who was looking back at him with a bit of concern on his face.

"Sure, sure. Come on in. Coffee?" Mike offered, before quickly looking at Max and snapping a finger, signaling the dog to lie down outside.

Lucinda had cleared the table and was getting mismatched coffee mugs down out of a cupboard. Mike quickly showed her where the Keurig pods were, in the next cupboard over, and turned to pull out a chair for the Sheriff who took it and sat down. Captain Trask followed suit and Mike took the third seat, leaving the padded bench seat along the wall for Lucinda, whom he wasn't sure was invited to this surprise meeting. She was one step ahead of him, serving first the Sheriff and then Trask a cup of coffee with a smile like she had done at the Thunderbird a thousand times, serving guests. She then served Mike before excusing herself to the back of the trailer where Mike figured she went to sit on his bed and listen, out of the way, at least physically.

The closeness of the two men, his supervisors, was uncomfortable. Travel trailers were not known for being spacious, and the kitchen table, although nice in this upscale brand, was small. He waited nervously, trying to show no pain from his shoulder wound as he took a sip of black coffee.

"Sergeant Taylor," the Sheriff began finally, taking off

his sunglasses, "So you're the hot shot California city cop I hired as a Sergeant, huh? The white cop that speaks Spanish and Lakota and who knows how many other languages, has all these slick schools under his belt, not one negative write-up in a ten year career, and a veteran to boot, comes here and starts doing big things! A joint investigation with the Sioux! First time I've seen that in my thirty years with the department! I get an accommodation request for you and Barton for a bang up job, which I just signed! Good work all around and a phone call from the TP Director of Public Safety thanking me for the investigation.

"So, imagine my surprise when I get a second call from him in a week expressing his regrets that my new sergeant was fucking shot on his reservation! Oh, and he went on to say that he was glad it wasn't a serious wound and hoped for your speedy recovery!

"Imagine how I felt not knowing what the fuck he was talking about! I call my Captain here who has allowed you to bivouac on his property, who recommended your hire, and he doesn't know what the fuck is going on either! So I told him to get in the truck and go for a ride with me.

"Don't you work tomorrow, sergeant?"

"Yessir," Mike said sheepishly.

"So when were you going to *enlighten us* on what in the Sam Hill happened?"

"I...I was just about to do that actually when I saw you pull up, sir."

"Mind telling us what happened, son? Give me the Reader's Digest abridged version since you are going to write this up in detail and turn it in directly to the Captain here. You know you are probationary? I can fire you any time without cause, and I have a lot of cause here! What were you doing out on the backside of the reservation anyway?"

Mike proceeded to give a short account of what happened, starting with going to sweat lodge at the property of a respected elder of the tribe and then getting hit in the shoulder while driving back, leaving out the real reason. He said it was all an accident and that the kids out plinking with their small bore rifles were real sorry about it. He added that the incident was reported and that a fellow TP officer he was friends with had taken him to the rez clinic for treatment and later brought his Tahoe home. He suggested he was good for at least desk duty starting tomorrow.

The Sheriff sat there thinking about it for a minute. The pause seemed like half an hour to Mike.

"You go to the sweat lodge with Indians? You don't just speak it, you believe in it too? Like that is church to you right? And answer very carefully son," the Sheriff said.

At that moment Mike knew he was going to be alright. The Sheriff was throwing him a life preserver in the form of religious activities.

"Yessir, I attend Native American religious activities. I have been a practitioner of Native American spirituality since I was ten years old."

"And your girlfriend there," he pointed with his thumb towards the back of the trailer, "she come with you from California or did you meet her here? I can't tell if she's Hispanic or Indian?"

"She lives on the rez sir, her parents own the Thunderbird Cafe. She is a graduate student at university and starts her Doctorate Program next week," Mike said, pride in his voice.

Both the Sheriff and Trask nodded their heads, impressed at this bit of information.

"As for you going to work tomorrow sergeant, you will not. Not until you go get me a note from a doctor on when you can return to limited duty and then full duty. You got that?"

"Yessir… can I ask one favor? If I can't return tomorrow could you have Deputy Yancy Rivera take roll call for me? She is ready to lead sir. I have been highly impressed with her abilities and professionalism."

"You are in no position to ask for favors, sergeant. I'll leave that up to Frank here. Thanks for the coffee. Nice rig you got here, always wanted one," the Sheriff said as he tilted his cup back, draining the last of his coffee, and then stood up to leave.

Frank Trask got up too.

"Thank you sir. I saved up for this puppy for several years, sir." Mike said.

The two men went outside to leave, Mike walking out

with them to watch them drive off when his cell phone notification tone went off in his pocket. It was Darth Vader's theme from Star Wars which caused both men to turn around, embarrassing Mike a bit. He usually put it on vibrate when at work so all his personalized ringtones couldn't be heard.

"Well, go ahead sergeant, answer it," Sheriff Tillerman said.

He fished his phone out of his pocket and noticed it was a text from an unknown number. He opened it quickly and read the short message:

[Wanted Camaro abandoned at Lakota Veterans memorial]

"Ah, it's a message from an unknown caller saying the Loller brother's Camaro is parked abandoned at the reservation Veteran's Memorial, sir."

The Sheriff turned and looked at Trask.

"Let's roll. It's not far from here. You can call it in on the way," he said to Trask as they got in the big Ford Expedition and left, kicking up dirt.

When Mike turned around, Lucinda was just inside the doorway.

"That was intense!" she said.

"You're telling me Luce! Looks like I have some phone calls to make. I need to call my insurance too and report this, see about getting it fixed and a loaner vehicle."

"You called me *Luce,*" she smiled, "Give me your

phone. I'll put in my number and get out of here so you can do what you have to do, but I'm bringing you dinner or taking you to the restaurant! I'm not working till you are back on your feet. My parents will be fine. I have to take care of my man."

"I like the sound of that!" he said with a grin.

As she left they hugged and kissed a right proper kiss, for a long time, tasting each other's mouths. They would be doing a lot of that in the next week before Lucinda went back to school. She was the best kisser Mike had ever had the pleasure of kissing.

As she drove off he realized that you don't always get the girl you want. That sometimes, just sometimes, Wakan Tanka gives you the girl you need.

Tribal Punishment

After what seemed like hours of driving, the vehicle finally came to a stop. Troy had dozed off again as he had several times, still suffering from the blow to the head. He was now more alert, better able to piece things together. He formulated a plan to escape. He really wanted to get this bag off his head just as soon as he was on his feet. He just couldn't figure out how these Indians had gotten the best of him. He knew there was something wrong with that phone call, but he had been desperate to get himself and his brother out of this. Stupid, he thought, just stupid of him to shoot that first guard. He should have just let it go.

The rear cargo door opened and he felt a pinch on his calf.

"Ouch!" he protested.

"This one's awake," said one of the voices.

"This one is still out. I think I thumped him too hard," said another.

"It was probably that second whack you gave him," said the third man.

Troy felt hands dragging him backwards out of the vehicle. They carried him several feet and then dropped his legs into some kind of hole. He couldn't see what was going on. It felt like a ledge. They lowered him down till his tied feet came in contact with the bottom. He was now lying at a steep angle as the hands pulled him upright into a standing position.

"Stand up!" one of them told him.

"What's going on?" he asked, realizing that maybe he wasn't going to be getting out of this afterall…

"Shut up! You'll find out in a minute!" an angry voice said.

He leaned forward and a hand held him as he stood. Then he heard what sounded like shovels scooping dirt as he felt a load of soft soil hit his feet.

Oh my god! Are they burying me? He thought as panic started to set in. His heart began to race, his breath coming now in quick short pants. The shoveling continued till it was up to his waist, at which point the hand let go of him. The shovels kept going and he felt the dirt rise up over his hands and past his chest. It became difficult to breathe.

"What the fuck! Can we talk about this?" he shouted, trying to bargain his way out of this, "I have information!"

"Good! We'll get to that in a minute," a voice said. It was the voice that had been talking about the white cop and the red and black roads, something later about tribal punishment… He hoped they were talking about him and his brother.

The shoveling slowed as they placed the last bit of dirt

around his neck, leaving only his head exposed. He heard the men doing the same to his brother–only he was unconscious. They talked about how they were going to bury him lying back at an angle, one man just holding him till the dirt did its job.

The potato sack was pulled off his head but he couldn't see his captors: they were standing behind him and it was dark. Out of his side vision, turning his head as far as he could in the dirt, he could see his brother's head sticking out of the earth some ten feet away. His head was lying back on the dirt, his mouth agape. Troy could see the dark colored Chevy Suburban parked a distance away.

"Now let's talk, my wasicu friend," the voice that liked whites said, "why did you shoot John LaVoy? My guess is that he saw something he wasn't supposed to see in that warehouse. Am I right? He wasn't supposed to go inside, was he?"

"You're in contact with Blackrock, ask them! They fucking sold me out, didn't they?" Troy shouted.

"Nope, they didn't sell you out. They have no idea where you are right now. But I suspect we're doing them a favor," the voice said.

"That doesn't make any sense! They called me, told me where to go to be extracted!"

"Answer the question. We'll get to that."

"Yeah, I shot the guard, he wasn't supposed to be in there, but everything's gone now, so it's all good."

"All good?" one of the other voices said, irritated, "It's all good to just shoot a pesky Indian isn't it?"

"This isn't about race, it's just business," Troy said, trying to take the prejudice off the issue, still trying to talk his way out of this.

"And who killed Janet Sweetwater? Was that you too? Nice piece of work that was by the way," the friendlier Indian asked.

"Yeah, I did that too, but that order came directly from Blackrock. Ask them; their number is on my phone. I take it you have that?"

"Yup, I got it. What's the name of your contact at this Blackrock agency? There isn't a listing for them that I can find. I take it that's a word-of-mouth outfit, vets only?"

"That's right. I got the number from a fellow Marine at the range. But you didn't answer my question. I mean how did you know I was going to be extracted and where to meet if you haven't been in contact with Blackrock? And I don't know any names! This is all black ops stuff for trained ex-military only!"

"Mmm, that's unfortunate," the voice said, "I called you. I told you where to go to be extracted. I got your number from your girlfriend, she was very helpful."

"Wait, what? Why would she talk to a Native American? You didn't hurt her did you? We have a kid!" Troy pleaded, panic refreshed.

"Oh, I'm one of the police officers that searched your

house there, Mister Troy Loller. She gave me your number and told me all about how Blackrock contacts you. It was pretty easy to fool you. You said yourself that my voice wasn't familiar to you. But you bit anyway."

Realization crept over his face like fire: he had been duped, and he wasn't getting out of this. He was going to die out here, wherever "here" was. His brother was probably in a coma and would never regain consciousness, which was probably a blessing considering the circumstances.

A man walked out in front of him dressed in traditional Lakota warrior clothing, his face painted. Takoda was smiling at him, holding a small hand drum in one hand and a traditional drumstick with a tan leather beater in the other. He knelt down to look Troy right in the eyes, began to drum softly on the hand drum, then sang a song in Lakota. It was the Kills-at-Night war song, but Troy had no way of knowing that. The men standing behind him joined in the song that seemed to repeat itself several times. At one point the Indian even stood and danced a bit, some war dance or something, kicking dust in his face.

Takoda finished his song and smiled down at Troy.

"Come on, boys, we're done here," Takoda said to the men behind Troy, a smile returning to his face.

"You can't just leave us here! I could work for you! Come on!" Troy begged.

"You can't just come here on our land and kill our people, wasicu! Did you really think you were going to get away with it?" said one of the other men.

"I...I was just following orders!" Troy said in defense.

"Yeah," Takoda began, "that didn't work for the Nazis at the Nuremberg Trials and it won't work for you either. That shit doesn't flush."

The men started walking to the Suburban.

"Hey, fuck you fucking Indians! Fucking Prarie Niggers! I'll get out of here and hunt you down!" Troy shouted.

"What did you say?" One of the men turned and drew a gun from his waistband and took aim, walking back towards the buried man.

The other two men also stopped and turned around.

"Let it go!" Takoda said with a commanding voice, "He's provoking you! He wants you to shoot him. Don't do it, brother. Don't let him off that easy."

The man stopped and lowered his gun reluctantly.

"I told myself that if any white ever called me that I would fucking kill him!" the man said.

"You are, brother. You are."

The man came back and they all got in the Suburban and drove off.

Troy listened to the big SUV as it drove off until all he could hear was the pounding of his heart in his ears. It was dark and all he could see were the stars above and maybe thirty feet in front of him. He looked over at his brother who didn't seem to even be breathing anymore. He began to struggle in the dirt and even made some progress loosening up the fresh soft soil. He could breathe better and turn his head and even his shoulders a bit. He wore himself out struggling, resting, and starting again. He was determined to get out of the dirt, help his brother and then seek his revenge on these men. But it was of little use. Without his hands he just couldn't lift himself up and out of the dirt. His legs and feet were anchored in good.

Then he heard something moving in the dark. Padded feet trotting along and then came to a stop. He heard sniffing and panting like a dog. *Thank God! Someone's dog!* he thought. Maybe there was someone nearby that would help him! A glimmer of hope came to him like a candle in the darkness.

"Hello! Help! I need help!" he shouted.

Nothing.

Even the dog had stopped panting momentarily while he shouted.

Then the dog yipped. It was a high-pitched yip. It yipped again and held the last note for a moment.

Troy came to a grim realization: this wasn't a dog at all. It was a coyote, and it had just called to the rest of its pack.

"No, no, no," he said to himself as the final panic set in.

In the distance, near and far, he heard the yips and howls of the rest of the pack answering the first dog, signaling him to yip again so they could find him, find the kill he had found for them all.

Other than the three men leaving in that SUV, there

wasn't another human soul within 30 miles of Troy Loller and his dying brother. No one to hear his screams.

Mike spent the day making phone calls and texts. He called personnel and got the number of the department's medical insurance, called and made an appointment. They wanted him to come right away after hearing he'd been shot, but he didn't have a car and made an appointment, some twenty miles away, for first thing in the morning. Plenty of time to get clearance to work at least light duty and make roll call. He called his insurance and spent what seemed like hours giving them the details of his crash. They wanted him to get a copy of the police report from the Tribal Police and fax that into them ASAP and to take his Tahoe to the closest dealership since he was now considered to be in a remote location. They also updated his address to that of Captain Trask's house address. He would have to talk to him about that until he could set up a post office box somewhere. He really didn't think all these things out when he moved here.

Mike went outside and tried to start his Tahoe. It started, barely, but he had to immediately shut it off as the radiator had been pushed back a bit and the fan was beating it hard– far more than just ticking. *Great*, he thought. He'd have to tow it. He looked up the closest GM dealership which was also a ways off but at least they had an Enterprise car rental attached to it. He didn't want to have to trouble Lucinda with a ride anywhere but he knew he may have to impose on her good nature.

As if on cue, he received a text from his beautiful curvy new girlfriend saying that rez radio had just reported that the Sheriff of Pine County himself had recovered the wanted Camaro of the Loller brothers, suspected in the recent killings on the reservation, at the Lakota Veterans Memorial. She added there was some discussion going on about jurisdiction and the Sheriff Department had just told rez radio in a phone interview that the Sheriff and one of his Captains had been working off of a tip and that there was an existing agreement that says Sheriff's Department personnel that see criminal activity on the rez, or who are in hot pursuit of a felon, can enter the reservation.

Mike knew the score here. The Sheriff wanted the glory of recovering the vehicle, and that was that. The brothers had dumped it and were in another vehicle: that was obvious. The car would be towed and gone over with a fine-toothed comb until the FBI would come in and seize it, but not until Barton and his boys got a good look at it. The case was officially closed once the feds stepped in and took it over but if the department could arrest the two brothers it would be a big one up on the feds, making them look bad.

It was around 2pm when Max growled and slipped outside through the flap in the door. Mike had been surfing the net and fell asleep, putting his head back on the couch and not daring to lay on his side just yet. The last thing he remembered was accepting Lucinda's friend request on Facebook before tilting his head back with a smile. When Max came back inside growling and nudged him, he knew he needed to get up and go look.

Then he heard two voices and laughter. It was coming from the other side of his trailer by his fire pit.

He looked out his kitchen window and saw two men sitting down in his own chairs right in front of his firepit.

"What the fuck?" he said to himself as he squinted to see better.

One of the men had long hair and was definitely Native. The other had shorter hair and looked like Takoda. He could see the man smiling from where he was and was pretty sure it was him. He was tempted to grab his Glock but left it as he went out and walked over to ascertain what exactly was going on without as much as a call or text. He figured Takoda was coming over to see how he was after the incident with Angry Boy and his friends. He didn't even know the names of the other two boys…

"Sergeant Mike Taylor!" Takoda said as he approached, "How are you feeling? Come on over here, I want you to meet somebody."

"Where the hell did you park? You could have called. Scared the crap out of me," he said.

"Over by the house," Takoda said, "We wanted to sneak up on you, Indian style, but that dog of yours gave us away didn't he? Well, that and us laughing at your fancy gas ring fire pit here."

"That's a good dog," the other man said.

The two men stood up as Mike approached them. Takoda was dressed in jeans and a button-up shirt. The other man wore faded jeans and a denim jacket, unbuttoned with a ribbon shirt underneath, a turquoise and red coral beaded necklace hanging from his neck. He looked very traditional, Mike thought. He was as tall as Mike and had a cunning look about him, like a predatory animal.

Max growled as he came up next to Mike's heel.

"Plotz," he said in German, commanding the dog to lie down.

Max complied immediately, resting his snout between his legs as he watched his master.

"Damn good dog!" the man said.

Mike shook hands with Takoda who then introduced the other man.

"Mike, this is Johnny, or John, Stands Outside. He is Angry Boy's uncle."

Mike tried to look natural. Even though on the inside he just switched from routine business with a friend to on-guard mode. He reached out to shake the man's hand. Johnny looked at Mike's outstretched hand for a moment and then shook it reluctantly.

"Sit. Let's talk," Takoda suggested.

"In the tradition of our peoples," Takoda began as the

men sat down on Mike's little camp chairs, "when there has been some offense committed by a member of the tribe, it was the tribe itself that determined the appropriate punishment. You may have noticed that when the Europeans came here to our land there were no jails, no prisons. We had no need for such things. We didn't use money or write down volumes of books to be stored in buildings either for that matter. The tribe decided what the punishment would be, what would be traded in compensation. The ultimate punishment was banishment that was almost always a death sentence to a brother. Without the tribe, a man alone was easy pickings to other tribes, animals, the elements, whatever. It is with this tradition in mind that we have decided what the punishment will be for the three youths that planned to kill you, wounded you and damaged your property. Since we are handling this all *in house,* so to speak. And we have you really to thank for that. So, thank you."

"Yes, pelameyaya," Johnny said in reluctant agreement.

"These boys did this on their own. They did not have any approval from any of their elders to do this. I want you to know that figured into this decision. They sometimes sweat with me and as a spiritual advisor I have failed them. I take some responsibility in this. Their families take some responsibility in this and they themselves take most of the responsibility in this.

"With this in mind, they will assist you in getting your Chevy fixed and driving you where you need to go, any shopping you need done or chores till you are back on your feet, which, I'm happy to see you already are by the way. How long will you be off of work?"

Mike digested this as he formulated an answer.

"I'm good. I go to the doc tomorrow morning and I'm hoping to be placed on light duty till I can go back on patrol. I guess I'm flattered by the offer but I'm good. I mean I need my Tahoe towed to the Chevy dealership for repairs today and a ride there so I can rent a car and all that, my deductible is five hundred bucks and I have a friend bringing me breakfast and dinner so that's about it. When I let those guys off the hook I just hoped they would get a good talking to by Funmaker and you."

Mike was careful not to mention Lucinda by name. He had no idea how that news would affect her or how these men viewed him for that matter. She may be in danger, at least to verbal ridicule for dating a white man, he suddenly realized. He did not want that for her at all. He knew Johnny was Angry Boy's uncle and what that meant. This man was a member of the Movement. He was a militant for all Mike knew, yet he was invited here and was sitting with Takoda, a Tribal Police Investigator. This was deep stuff. He really didn't want any part of it. He was happy to sweat once a week and go to work, dating his Native American girl.

"Oh they did, believe me. And it's not over yet!" Takoda said, "What do you say, John?"

Johnny Stands Outside sat and thought for a moment, shook his head.

"You know who I am?" he said in Lakota, looking directly at Mike.

"Yes," Mike answered in Lakota, "I know who you are. I have no problem with you or your people. I am new here. I may speak Lakota a little, but I am not First Nations, not one drop of my blood is Native American. But I have practiced your religion by choice since I was a boy. I would like to continue to go to lodge once a week and go to work, that is all."

Johnny looked at Takoda and then back at Mike, nodding his head in agreement.

"I do not like white people. But, I can tolerate you. I do like your dog," he smiled.

All three men looked over at Max, who raised his head in response to the sudden attention.

Johnny stood up and reached in his front jeans pocket and withdrew a wad of one hundred dollar bills. He counted out five and handed them to Mike.

"I will have a tow truck here in thirty minutes," Johnny said, speaking English now, "they will take it to the dealership for you. You will have a car with a full tank of gas to drive in a couple of hours. Don't worry, it's not stolen. Call Takoda if you need any errands run and he will have Raymond or one of the others do it. Let's keep their phone numbers off of your phone records. And if you ever need to reach me just call Takoda. He knows how to get a hold of us."

Mike knew exactly what *us* meant. It meant *The Movement.*

Sure enough, 45 minutes after they left, a tow truck arrived and hooked up Mike's Tahoe. The Native American driver had a garage-like uniform shirt on with a clipboard and everything, all very professional and normal-looking as he had Mike sign a form and tore off the back copy and gave it to him, said to call the dealership and let them know he was coming in case he needed to give permission to start work on the vehicle.

An hour after that, just after getting a text from Lucinda asking him if it was dinner for two at the trailer or the Thunderbird, two cars came down the road and pulled up to the gate and stopped. He recognized the lead car as Raymond Angry Boy Whitecloud's classic Monte Carlo. Raymond got out of his car and stood at the gate.

Mike told Max to stay and walked down to the gate where he could see one man, older than Raymond, sitting in the second car looking at him.

"Hao Kola," Mike said.

"Hao," Raymond said, intentionally leaving the Kola (*friend*) out of it, "Here's my car. I took my stuff out and it's full. It's old so when you start it just pump the gas to the floor twice, then turn the key. Otherwise it will just crank and crank."

"Oh wow, I didn't think I would be driving your car? It's well taken care of. What year is it?" Mike asked, trying to build rapport.

"It's an '88. Last year they made it, till they started up again in '95, but those are crap!"

"I'll be careful with it. I should only have it for as long as it takes to get my Tahoe fixed. Sorry you have to part with it. Do you have something else to drive?"

"I didn't have much of a choice. Yeah, I have other cars. I'm a mechanic. I built that car in high school auto shop. Well, I'll see you around then," he said and walked over to the passenger side of the following vehicle and left without another word: without asking him how his shoulder was or thanking him for keeping him out of jail.

Mike watched them drive off. He figured the boy, an adult by legal standards, was just embarrassed by his punishment and didn't want to face him so soon after the incident. He opened the gate and proceeded to search the car, including under the hood and in the trunk. It was just an automatic response to Mike, just like he searched every police car he got in even if he knew and trusted the previous officer or deputy. He was trained to search the car and be sure nothing was left inside that a suspect could use against him and, as a matter of record, if he found something dumped in a unit after transporting an arrestee. In this case he was more interested in weapons – or a bomb.

The car was clean other than a faint odor of marijuana.

"Everything okay, Mike?" Captain Trask's wife asked.

Mike hadn't noticed she'd come down—he was too busy searching the vehicle and fighting the painful protests of his wounded shoulder. She was probably worried upon hearing that their new resident had been shot by Native Americans.

"Yes ma'am, everything is great. Just checking out this old Monte Carlo before I drive it. It's a loaner from my rez pals."

"That boy looked like he was sixteen years old! Was he one of the boys that shot you by accident? That man in the other car must have been his dad. He didn't look happy," she said.

"He was. His name is Raymond Angry Boy Whitecloud. This is his car. His...relatives are making him loan it to me till my Tahoe is fixed. It's a tribal punishment, very traditional."

"Oh," she said, "we'll come out later and have a cocktail with you. I want to hear about what happened. Frank said you almost got sacked over it!"

"Yeah, that was not fun. I'll be going to the Thunderbird with Lucinda for dinner and then we'll be back. I'll tell you all about it."

"Oh, have you met a girl already?" she asked with a coy smile.

"Yes ma'am, I have."

Lucinda picked Mike up a few minutes after 4pm from the front of the gate: he had been waiting for her there since she texted him that she was on her way. She saw Angry Boy's car immediately and asked what it was doing there, and if he was there...with concern in her voice. He proceeded to tell her of his afternoon since she'd left. She sucked in breath so hard and looked at him while driving so many times he had to tell her to watch the road. She was not happy about the visitors he had, saying they were bad medicine with the exception of Takoda, who always tried to keep the peace as a spiritual man and police officer. Mike said he didn't bring up her name at all out of fear they wouldn't like her dating him. She just drove for a good few minutes after that, not knowing what to say. She changed the subject to what he wanted to eat.

They ran into Sergeant War Club at the cafe, of course, as it was his time of day to eat dinner there and he chided them about dating in a friendly way. They took a booth next to him as he was about done anyway. Mike asked him if there was any information on the Loller brothers and he smiled and didn't answer right away. As he got up to go pay the bill he leaned over next to their head level.

"I heard they are resting with Unhcegila now," he whispered and smiled, before walking away.

It was Mike's turn to go a little pale. His heart picked up a few beats as he looked into Lucinda's big questioning brown eyes.

"What is it?" she asked him, "Unhcegila, that's the giant serpent god, right? Killed by the magic arrows the twins shot her with?"

"Yes, although there are a few versions of Unhcegila and how she was killed. One version is that she fell to earth gravely wounded, thrashed around for years dying, damaging the land where she lay forever. Some believe that's how the badlands were formed."

"The badlands over on Pine Ridge?" she asked.

"Yes, the same. This is deep. I'm not going to repeat this story to anyone at the department. You know what this means don't you?"

"That one of my people caught them and did them in?"

"Yes, one or more... I don't think they abandoned their car at the veterans memorial. I think it was dumped there by whoever found those two brothers. I think they're dead and the FBI will have them on their most wanted lists for many years. This is deep stuff. I don't want to know any more about it. I don't know what I got myself into moving here!" he said.

"Well, you met me," she smiled.

"Yes," he smiled, "one really good thing! Thank Tunkashila for that!"

They ordered and got into a chit-chat about her being a Catholic Native American and him being a wasicu who knows all the Lakota Wakanpi spirits and divinities. This would be one of a thousand conversations they would have in the months to come. He thought of telling her it wasn't safe for them to date after what had happened, but dismissed it. This was the one good thing that had happened in his life and he didn't want to let it go. Still, he told her maybe she shouldn't change her status on Facebook to *in-a-relationship* just yet: let that info go out into the world slowly, the old-fashioned way. For as much as he fancied the idea of his pals back home seeing that he was in a relationship with Lucinda (who's profile photo was amazing), he could wait. He didn't need revenge on his ex that bad. Thoughts of her faded with each new day.

Their food arrived and Lucinda said her Catholic prayer and made the sign of the cross. He smiled and thanked Wakan Tanka for his food so the Wo Nagi would be satisfied that he was considerate of the spiritual essence of all food that comes from mother earth.

"Who did you pray to?" she asked with a cute smile.

"He's really the same god you know," he said.

"You're such an Indian," she replied.

Rumor Control

L ucinda was there bright and early with breakfast, but un-like the day before, Mike was able to get himself up early and go about his morning routine before she arrived. This was difficult since he couldn't stop thinking about her. So, when she came in the door, it seemed like she had just left. They had been making out on the couch like teenagers till 10pm when she announced she had to either leave or spend the night. He didn't mind. It was a refreshing feeling–like he was back in highschool. He knew she wasn't ready for any heavy physical contact yet and he was not only willing but happy to wait for her. It sure was going to be epic when they finally decided to take that next step, he mused, but not yet: he couldn't perform to standard with his current injuries.

She left after breakfast and coffee with minimal kissing so he could get to his appointment on time.

The Monte Carlo started up just fine after two pumps of the gas pedal, just like Angry Boy had instructed. Mike looked at the route on his phone once before turning the volume all the way up so he could hear directions to the doctor's office. He'd had food and coffee and was topped

Michael Max Darrow

out on Motrin and Tylenol and was ready to put on a show for the doc–or so he thought.

"Nope, no way," the young Filipino doctor said, "you need at least a week of rest before I let you go on light duty. You cannot shrug your shoulders or raise your arm to shoulder level even."

Mike had tried, but the doc wasn't going to be fooled or persuaded otherwise. He was lucky the doc let him out of physical therapy due to his remote location, after promising to do the simple exercises he would be shown after a week of no movement and in a sling. The doc made him get another x-ray before he left as he hadn't thought to have a copy of the films from the rez clinic sent over. Now Mike would have to inform the department that he was going to miss some time at work after all. He was close and decided to just drive over there rather than call–he had a note from the doctor to turn in anyway.

He parked in the back lot and entered through the back door to avoid the watch commander, not knowing who was on duty at the moment. He found Frank in his office talking to Yancy Rivera. They were both surprised to see him.

"Mike! So are you coming to work today after all?" Frank asked, skeptically, "I just told Deputy Rivera here she would be doing roll call for you for a while."

"She will," Mike answered, "I'm off for a week, then light duty and physical therapy until the doc is satisfied I can hop, skip and jump again."

234

"That's what I thought. I have the relief lieutenant going on vacation next week so that will work out just fine.
You can be the acting relief watch commander for a few
weeks and then we'll see how you are doing. You got that
report on the shooting for the Sheriff for me? And attach a
copy of the rez PD's report to that also, would ya?"

"Yessir, I'm working on it."

"Emailed to me by 1400 hours – today!" Frank said,
all business now, not letting on to Rivera that Mike was a
friend.

Mike excused himself and went downstairs to check
his box. He wasn't going to make Yancy do his paperwork.
He could do that. She caught up with him in the hall, saying
she needed to talk to him. He suggested they go outside to
their vehicles.

"Who's car is this?" she asked, looking at the nice old
Monte Carlo.

"It's a loaner from a rez friend. Long story," he
answered.

"Yeah, there's a lot of long stories about you swirling
around at the moment, another one every day! What the
fuck happened? We're hearing you got shot by Indians and
that you were trespassing or another version is that you are
seeing some young squaw and her relatives ran you off! We
heard you almost got fired by Tillerman himself but you
knew where that fucking Camaro was so he made a trade
with you. That one doesn't make any sense at all, by the

way. The twins started a betting pool that you won't make it to the end of the month! Care to share with me what's going on so I can set them straight? Thank you for roll call by the way. Captain Trask said you specifically asked for me to cover for you. That was really cool of you, Army."

"What am I up to?" Mike asked.

"What?"

"The pool. How many bucks am I up to?" he asked.

"Thirty four dollars. Stop stalling. Tell me what happened!" she demanded in her Marine Corps way.

"Well, it's pretty simple really. I was driving off the rez after going to sweat lodge at an elder's house and some youngsters were out plinking at cans and I got hit in the trap and ended up in a ditch. I made a report and that is that. As for the Native American lady I am seeing, she is twenty two and a graduate student, so there. *Squaw* is really not a word I thought I would hear coming out of your mouth Yancy. That's like calling you a chola."

"I *am* a chola. Well, I was. Not my word, just the rumor, sorry. And that Camaro? The girl has cleared out by the way. Loller's pad is empty."

"I can imagine. You guys probably roll by the residence twenty times a shift!"

"Those fuckers shot at us! That's another rumor floated by Ahern, that maybe you got in a shootout with the Lollers and found their car but didn't want to report it because you were off duty and on the rez."

"Wow! You guys have been busy with the rumor mill! Nope, I got an anonymous phone call telling me where the car was. Tillerman and Trask were at my trailer when the call came in. But I think that saved my job. That and the fact that I was on the rez for religious purposes. He came out there to fire me. I'm on probation, no cause needed."

"Fuck me. I might make sergeant after all!" she smiled, "But who would have your phone number?"

"I have no idea? I think the TP put it out on rez radio when we started the joint investigation," he lied, "How much did you put in the pool?"

"Two bucks."

Mike spent the rest of the day making calls and writing that report for the Sheriff. He emailed Takoda and asked him to attach a copy of Tully's report as soon as possible so he could attach it to his report that was due in a few hours. Takoda responded in minutes saying he would go pull it and scan it and by the time Mike was done with the report he had the email. He attached the PDF of Tully's report to his document on the incident and emailed it to Frank.

Lucinda going back to school had been a real bummer for both Mike and Max. They had gotten quite used to seeing her on a daily basis. Her voice, her positive attitude, not to mention her beauty, had very much affected them. The old Airstream seemed cold and empty now.

Mike rested his shoulder dutifully for that first week before going to Physical Therapy for some papers on what exercises to do daily and getting that note from the doc allowing him to go back to work. He did the arm raises and shrugs till the pain stopped him several times a day and was making some good progress. There was a little catch in his trapezius now due to muscles being permanently damaged, causing scar tissue in the fibers that might or might not get better with time.

There were follow-up questions from the Sheriff's Office on his report and he got a call from one of the FBI agents that he met at the Loller place that day they were serving the warrant. Both had to do with the anonymous phone call: both times he repeated the lie that he *thought* rez radio had put his phone number out there. He was hoping neither party would actually get federal warrants and listen to the hours and days involved in all those recordings since the incident began. If they did, and found no mention of his phone number with a 714 Santa Ana area code, he was going to have a lot of explaining to do that he simply was not up for. He could just imagine how that conversation would go–*Oh, well, I'm friends with some Tribal Police that have some sort of working relationship with the militant wing of the Native American Movement. I sort of met with them too. No big deal.* Yeah, he thought, that would be swell.

His Tahoe was almost ready; he just needed to arrange a ride to the dealership in a few days to pick it up. Luckily, the frame had not been bent. They did have to replace both front fenders, a bumper, the fan and fan housing, and the radiator, then match the paint on the new fenders. He really didn't want to have Takoda call Johnny Stands Outside to have him direct someone to come give him a ride. He decided he'd have Lucinda take him on the weekend–the dealership was open on Saturdays. Lucinda hadn't come home the first weekend back at school saying she had too much to do to get ready for the semester and was taking on some teacher's aid assignments as well. He hoped this was not a bad sign. But, when he did see her, she was so happy to see him that his fears were assuaged and the kissing resumed late into the nights.

Mike was back to work in no time and although it was boring, not being in the field, he had to laugh: in being wounded and almost fired he had actually gotten a bit of a promotion, albeit temporary, working as an acting watch commander which he realized was just like being a sergeant–just not mobile. He did have to see the brass walking around throughout the station during the day shift but he just acted like he was reading. They all seemed to enjoy looking at him, probably due to his reputation as an upstart Lakota-speaking oddity who had just been shot, on the reservation no less, but he was getting used to it. He just wanted to get back into the field. He stopped by roll call for his team whenever he worked that watch.

After two weeks he had his Tahoe back and decided on a whim to drive out to Funmaker's place, on a Wednesday, to see if the old man had continued with the inipi Ceremonies. Mike did not have Funmaker's phone number. The old man wasn't a *let's-exchange-numbers* kind of guy, but Mike wanted to talk to him about a good many things. They had started a journey together, restarting the lodge and he wanted very much to continue that. He also wanted to ease into a conversation on Phil Velardi and if Funmaker was related to him. From what he had seen and heard, from how they had built the lodge together to Funmaker's offhanded comments about Phil and those of others, he was pretty sure Funmaker was Phil's uncle–or dad even.

It was a bit surreal driving back out there. He felt like he was disobeying orders or trespassing or something, and when he drove past the spot where he had been shot, he stopped and looked at the tracks on the lip of the wash. He saw where he had parked and the place he went over the side. It brought chills to his skin to look at it; the memory of it made his shoulder twinge with pain for the first time in days. He could see the place where a tow truck had winched his Tahoe up and out of the wash, many footprints on the ground all over the entire area.

When he pulled up onto the little plateau where Funmaker's trailer sat, he saw Tully's Jeep and a few other cars. The fire was already lit and the men were sitting inside the grounds near the sacred mound. Funmaker got up and walked out to him, leaving his two old friends and another man sitting with his head down, covered with a towel as if in deep thought. There was something familiar about the man, but he was in his underwear and a T-shirt with his head covered so Mike just couldn't quite place him. Tully was tending the fire and looked over at him without making a single expression. He knew the big man had to know he was dating Lucinda by now and didn't want to have that conversation with him, knowing how he disapproved of such matches. He'd probably damaged that relationship for good. Too bad, he thought. He really liked Tully.

"You're late, white man. We already lit the fire. Are you going to sweat?" Funmaker asked, walking up as Mike got out of his Tahoe.

"Well, no. I didn't know if you were having a lodge today and didn't have your number. I didn't bring my stuff. Who is that with the towel on his head? He looks familiar," he asked.

"What *stuff?* You're wearing underwear aren't you?" Funmaker said, turning to look at the man with the towel covering his head, "Oh, that's Takoda. You probably didn't recognize him not wearing a suit!"

"Oh. I thought he did his own lodges on Sundays? And yes, I'm wearing skivvies! I mean my bag, my tobacco and prayer feather, change of clothing and my wash cloth, water…"

"He does. He's kind of doing a special sweat, a healing.

You know, recent events which we won't talk about here. There is a water hose over there," he pointed, "Go into the house and get a towel or washcloth or whatever, next to the bathroom in the cupboard. Come on, I'll smudge you in."

Funmaker turned and walked back to the grounds, leaving Mike to make the decision whether to sweat or not to sweat...

It will be sweat, he decided, and went in to get a towel and washcloth, then walked over to the grounds where the two older men started teasing him immediately, saying things about the wasicu with a hole in him and all things related to being shot by Indians and coming back for more. He laughed it off and suddenly felt really good. It was good to be back. He said hello to both Takoda and Tully; Takoda didn't answer, deep in thought, and Tully just grunted.

"Is it okay if I come in with you?" he asked Takoda.

"Ohan," (yes) he said, keeping his head down.

Mike didn't push it any further. He figured Takoda was having some bad thoughts and was trying to get back on the Red Road. He wondered if Takoda knew anything about the demise of the Loller brothers, knowing his working relationship with the movement, but this was not the time to ask.

"He's seeing a Lakota girl now too!" Tully said, walking over after fixing the fire.

Here we go, Mike thought.

"Oh yea?" one of the older men said.

"No," said the other, but smiled.

"It's okay," Tully said, "She started the flirting. She probably would have married a wasicu anyway."

He sat down next to where Mike was standing, stripping down to his boxers and shirt. Mike was relieved to hear Tully say that as he sat down and gingerly bent over to remove his shoes and socks.

When he took off his T-shirt, with some effort, the men, all but Takoda, looked at his bullet wounds.

"Oh, you a holy man now too. Maybe you should lead lodge?" one of the older men said, which garnered a lot of laughter. Even Takoda chuckled under his towel.

"Fire is ready. Let's go in and smoke the pipe," Funmaker said in Lakota.

After lodge, Mike sat on the ground next to a flowing water hose, drinking a ton of water and letting it flow over his head. He was a little shaky and felt exhausted. He hadn't done his camel routine before the lodge and it showed, his muscles cramping a bit already. He remembered one time that he drove too early after a lodge in Temecula, California and his foot cramped on the 215 freeway and he had almost crashed. He knew he would have to wait a while before driving home to the Airstream. He wasn't worried about Max. The Trasks had practically adopted the spoiled dog, playing fetch with him daily and giving him so many treats he was going to have to go on a diet.

Takoda was the first to leave, waving to Mike after shaking everyone's hands. It was a work day for Takoda and Mike didn't know if he had to go back to work or if he had taken a day off?

The two older men left, also waving to him and saying it was a good lodge and see you next week. They were nice old-timers. Mike decided it was time to get their names next week. Tully waited till the fire was completely out like a good fire tender and then sat down next to Funmaker.

Mike got himself up with some effort and walked over to them, dripping water with a shaggy muddy butt. This was something that would be disturbing to most folk but to those that attended sweat lodge it was a fairly common occurrence. Sitting on dirt and sweating profusely almost always caused this to happen. Dousing oneself with a garden hose for fifteen minutes just amplified the effect.

"So, Michael," Funmaker began, "tell us about this Native girl you are seeing. Is it serious?"

"I think so. I think I'm going to marry her, but knowing Lucinda, we will live on the rez and have ten kids and that's fine with me."

"Lucinda? That's a Spanish name. What do her people call her?" Funmaker asked.

"Chapawee, because she is a busy girl, college girl,"

Tully answered before Mike could, "Her parents own the Thunderbird Cafe."

"Ah, I haven't seen her since she was a little girl. Always talking and smiling, that one. Washte Michael, washte," Funmaker said.

"She wants to do something on the rez to help her people when she finishes college. She is full of facts and figures. She likes to tell me how many Lakota there are, about 70 thousand, and that three quarters of them live off the reservation, only half speaking their native language and most all living below the national poverty level. She wants to work with children."

Both men shook their heads in approval.

"I have a question for you Uncle," Mike said, turning to Funmaker, "Phil Velardi, he is your son? Maybe it is time that he came home?"

Funmaker thought about that for a moment.

"You'll have to ask him that," he said.

"I will give him a call. He should be with his people," Mike said.

"He can't use his real name, but he could return now, I think," Tully said.

Reflections

Months later, as the snow melted away and the weather turned towards spring, Mike flexed his healed shoulder reflexively as he sat at the Thunderbird Cafe waiting for Sergeant War Club to arrive. He was running a bit late due to a property dispute on the rez. Mike sat there drinking iced tea in the rear booth, reflecting on the past months since moving to South Dakota. Who would have thought that moving out here would have led to such an adventure? When he'd left the big city life in Santa Ana he thought he was heading to the great outdoors of law enforcement, so to speak. Things were supposed to be slower out here, and for the most part they were.

Mike's mind raced with all that had happened: the incident with the Loller brothers (still wanted by the FBI, a wanted poster still hanging on the bulletin board outside the roll call room) the corruption on the rez with L & M Logistics (now gone with another company in its place), meeting Lucinda, the Pow Wow and all that went with moving out here.

It took a month for that extremely thorough young doctor to let him go back on full duty. Truth be told, he knew he hadn't been ready even then. He had been in considerable pain raising his left arm over his head, but he kept acting like everything was peachy keen. He was back on full duty after two weeks of being the relief watch commander, followed by a few weeks of working either in dispatch in the made up position of "communications supervisor" or being an extremely overqualified desk officer on day shift when the lobby was open. He was glad to get back to supervising his shift, running roll call, and reading reports. The practical jokes had resumed almost immediately with no sign of relent. It was all good fun and he gave as good as he got. Putting a stuffed bobcat he'd found at a garage sale in one of the twins' patrol cars on the back ramp before roll call was definitely a hit with the troops.

Yancy Rivera finally made sergeant when a Lieutenant retired and another sergeant moved up. She was now working in the relief spot and Mike considered her a friend and staunch ally on the department.

Things couldn't be better with Lucinda. She and Mike had fallen deeply in love with each other and when it felt right, it felt right. She was moving home in a few days to continue her education–mostly online. They had spent every weekend together and he went up there to spend at least one day a week with her during the semester and well, one thing had led to another and they talked of getting married and then finding a place to live. Her father and mother met Mike after a month and seemed to like him, though he didn't know if this was their Catholicism or they really were happy for their only industriously busy little girl. They had offered a portion of their ten acres of property on the rez for Mike and Lucinda to build a house and move his trailer there in the meantime. But, he didn't want to rush things. Mike knew Luce wanted a Catholic wedding and all but he still wanted to do something traditional as well...

Mike had called his old spiritual leader, Phil Verardi, and spoke with him about the old man named Tom Funmaker. Phil went quiet as soon as Mike mentioned his name, listening as Mike laid out how they had built a lodge together and how he had started sweating with the old man and his friends, adding a few new friends until he got to the part about him being shot by a few kids. Phil was suddenly very concerned for Mike's safety on the rez and seemed to know there was more to the story, asking a lot of probing questions. Mike told him that if he came for a visit he would tell him more in person. Mike told him that even his new friends on the Tribal Police said it was safe for him to return, but he should continue to use the name Phil Velardi. Hell, Mike didn't even know his real name. And that was fine.

Hobby finally arrived, snapping him out of his reveries.

"Sorry about that," he began, "someone built a new fence and there was an issue over a few inches or feet or whatever. I got it all worked out for now, hopefully. So, Lucinda is coming home for good I hear. You guys set a date yet?"

"No. We're in no hurry and her parents aren't pushing her either, which is nice. Being Catholic, I thought they would want us to walk down the aisle before moving in together, but they are okay with it. I'd still like to do something traditionally Lakota too…"

"You've met her parents a few times now, right? Aren't you glad her mom goes home at 2 o'clock? That would have been embarrassing finding out that the waitress taking your order for months was Lucinda's mom!" he chuckled.

"I know, right? Luce says her mom likes to wait tables for exercise and to know the customers and the business. Her dad only comes in for about an hour a day to do inventory and order stuff. Yes, I've been to the house. It's nice inside. Very South Western. Her dad asks me lots of questions about lodge. He used to go when he was young. I think he would have gone the traditional route himself if not for his wife being very into the Catholic church, bake sales, committees and all that."

They ordered food before resuming the conversation.

"You could always buy her dad five horses for his daughter. That's what they did in the old days. If he accepts the gift, you're married. Simple as that," Hobby suggested.

"Oh yeah, that would go over like a lead balloon! Horses require a lot of money to keep and they don't have any horses now, and Luce would never let me hear the end of it, 'Is that all I'm worth is five horses?' Great idea!"

"Well, I know they need a new dishwasher for the

restaurant. This one keeps breaking down and they cost about four grand. You could buy them a new one and say you want to help out if you are going to be part of the family by marrying their only daughter. That would satisfy the *Traditional gift* side of things. Nice uniform shirt by the way. Is that new? That your commendation medal for the joint investigation?" Hobby asked.

Mike thought about what he suggested. Four thousand dollars was a lot of money but he had it. It was a lot more than rounding up five wild mustangs to give but it would be a nice gesture, especially if they were going to live in the Airstream behind their home and build a place…

"Yeah, this is a new shirt and yes, this is for the joint investigation" he said, tapping the enameled metal rectangle shaped ribbon pinned on his shirt above the pocket, "Barton got one too. I'll think about that industrial dishwasher. That's a good idea. I can do it as a gift to help out, if I'm going to be part of the family."

"There ya go!" Hobby said, pausing, "You know, something has been bugging me that I want to talk to you about."

"What's that?" Mike asked.

"You remember when we met, that first day, and we were standing out there by the body of John LaVoy? You on one side of the fence, me and Tully on the other side of the fence and Tully asked you who your people were–do you remember that?"

"Yeah sure," Mike answered.

"Do you remember what your answer was? You said that you don't have any. Do you remember that? That's been bugging me."

"Well I'm kind of an odd duck I've always thought. When I was a kid and I started on the Red Road I didn't know it was going to put me in between two cultures, two different ways of life. I've never felt like I fit in," Mike said.

"We're friends right?" Hobby asked, "Tully is your friend in his moody brooding way, Takoda and Funmaker are your friends, Lucinda is going to be your wife. What I'm saying is that we are your people now. Your friends are your people. The people you can count on. The people you can trust. Hell, that's what Lakota means! So, I don't want to hear that, 'I don't have any people' anymore. As far as I'm concerned, you are Lakota."

Mike didn't know what to say. He smiled and looked down at the table, wishing their food would arrive so he wouldn't have to talk for a while. What Hobby just said to him warmed his soul, made him feel really good and a little embarrassed at the same time.

"So," he said, looking up at Hobby, "would you consider being my Best Man?"

Epilogue

A few months later, people were arriving at the First Annual Pine County/Big Pine Law Enforcement Family Picnic. Held at a big park with a lot of swing sets, slides and jungle gym-like sets for the kids to play on, Lucinda and her mom helped organize the incoming food and potluck items under a gazebo, Lucinda looking very beautiful.

It was a good showing. The Sheriff didn't show, but several sergeants and a lieutenant, Captain Trask and his wife, along with their counterparts from the Tribal police showed up.

Several officers and deputies attended, their kids running off to start playing, making new friends without regard or thought of where they lived or what race the grown ups and governments categorized them as. The adults grouped by race for the most part, which was to be expected, but they were there; it was a start. Even Sergeant Rivera showed up, on duty, in the Supervisor's SUV for a while, got a plate of food and chatted a bit before she had to go back in service.

Mike felt good about the gathering. He was talking to Hobby and Tully when Takoda arrived and waved for Mike to come out to the parking lot. He walked over and asked what was up, to which Takoda promptly fished out a stack of papers from a box in his backseat and handed them to Mike.

They were missing persons posters with pictures of two young teenage Native American girls on the front with their information and a toll free number to call if they were seen or located.

Takoda asked Mike if he could distribute them at the Sheriff's Department, post them and pass them out at roll calls. Of course, Mike readily accepted. Takoda explained that too many Native American girls and children went missing on reservations all over the nation on an annual basis. Mike took the posters and put them in his Tahoe with Takoda following him. He said in the future he would just email him every time a new poster was generated if that was okay. Mike said that was great and that he had no idea there was such a problem.

Together, they walked up and joined the picnic.

References

National Native American Law
Enforcement Association, (NNALEA)
www.nnalea.org 202-204-3065

First Nations Development Institute
www.firstnations.org 303-774-7836

Native American Rights Fund, (NARF)
www.narf.org 303-447-8760

National Indigenous Women's Resource
Center, (NIWRC)
www.niwrc.org 406-477-3896

Acknowledgements

The author would like to recognize the following individuals for their help, suggestions and Beta reading of this novel before publication.

Michelle R. (The Boss) Darrow
Barry (Bear) Clay
Mary (The Colonel) Bennett Johnson

Editor
Alex Eastly, alex.eastly@gmail.com

About the Author

Michael Max Darrow was born in Southern California where he lives with his wife of 30 years. They have three adult children. He served his country, joining the military right out of high school, then later in the National Guard as a Commissioned Infantry Officer. He also served his community as a Police Officer until he retired.

Michael has also worked as a Private Investigator and as an Executive Protection Specialist. He has a Black Belt in Tang Soo Do, also studying the Samurai Sword and Philipino Stick Fighting.

He is a proud member of the Ancient and Honorable Order of E Clampus Vitus, a fraternal organization dedicated to the history of the Old West, the State of California and the Gold Rush. He is also a member of the American Legion.

www.michaelmaxdarrow.com

Made in United States
Cleveland, OH
14 April 2025

16101379R00148